THE CLANDESTINE CORONER

THE CLANDESTINE CORONER

A FENWAY STEVENSON NOVELLA

PAUL AUSTIN ARDOIN

PRAISE FOR THE CLANDESTINE CORONER

Curl up in your favorite chair with a cup of joe, because you won't be able to stop reading this fast-paced, clever murder mystery.

C.B. SAMET, BESTSELLING AUTHOR OF
THE DR. LILLIAN WHYTE ADVENTURES

A brilliant whodunit with plenty of twists—and a great cast of characters that made me want to read the whole series!

ANGELA C. NURSE, AUTHOR OF
THE ROWAN MACFARLANE MYSTERIES

PRAISE FOR PAUL AUSTIN ARDOIN

Be warned: to read one Fenway mystery is to want to read them all. If you love page-turning, unputdownable mysteries, then Ardoin is the real deal.

MARK STAY, HOST OF
THE BESTSELLER EXPERIMENT PODCAST

Think Sue Grafton and Janet Evanovich, but with darker twists and more biting social commentary.

JOHN LING, USA TODAY BESTSELLING AUTHOR

This is as good a mystery series as you will find in print. You do not want to miss a single one of these books.

DAVID MARVIN, SCINTILLA BOOK REVIEWS

THE CLANDESTINE CORONER

Copyright © 2022 by Paul Austin Ardoin

Published by Pax Ardsen Books

This book is a work of fiction. Names, characters, businesses, organizations, places, events and incidents either are the product of the author's imagination or are used fictitiously. Any resemblance to actual persons, living or dead, events, or locales is entirely coincidental.

ISBN 978-1-949082-41-8

For information please visit:

www.paulaustinardoin.com

Cover design by Ziad Ezzat of Feral Creative Colony: feralcreativecolony.com

AUTHOR'S NOTE

This story takes place between the events of *The Accused Coroner* (Book Seven of *The Fenway Stevenson Mysteries*) and *The Offside Coroner* (Book Eight).

CHAPTER ONE

Fenway Stevenson knelt as she snapped on her blue nitrile gloves. The warm light from the crystal chandeliers gleamed off the oiled parquet floor. Behind the man's bald head, the congealing pool of blood shimmered, crimson against the wood.

The dead man, lying on his back in the middle of the ballroom, was perhaps in his late fifties. Clean-shaven, with a thin face and pointed features; pale, almost pinkish skin; small brown eyes set far apart, mouth slightly open, thin lips and small teeth. Perhaps—Fenway glanced over his thin frame—five foot seven. The man wore gray trousers, a crisp white dress shirt, and a tie in a light purple, almost lavender, with the letters "MB" embroidered near the bottom of the tie, right in the center.

Behind Fenway, Sergeant Dez Roubideaux paced back and forth, the lights above combining with the early evening sun through the windows, a cacophony of her shadows scattering across the floor.

"You okay?"

"I've never been in this building." Dez bent down to grab the roll of crime scene tape. "I'll cordon the room off?"

"In a minute." Fenway squinted at the shiny pool of blood. "Any witnesses?"

"No one's talking so far," Dez answered, folding her arms, the roll of tape still in her hand. "I've cornered all three of the members who are still here, but they're giving me nothing."

"They refuse to answer your questions?"

"That's right. All three of them gave me the same quote." Dez set the roll of yellow tape back on the floor and opened her notebook. "'Debate shall be among those ye trust, and let no man outside these walls discover secrets between the brethren.' Sort of sounds like the King James Version, but it's no verse I know."

"Or maybe their employee handbook was written by someone who liked Elizabethan English." Fenway gingerly lifted the victim's head off the floor, the blood sticky. "If they're quoting arcane texts when you ask them simple questions, it's useless to try to get them to talk."

"Maybe they didn't think we'd show up so fast."

"What do they expect? The coroner's office is only a few blocks away." She turned the dead man's head, then craned her neck down to look at the wound.

Dez crouched about five feet behind the pool of blood. "No ID?"

"No wallet, anyway. Hasn't been dead long—he's still warm. Keys were in his right pants pocket. One is for a BMW."

"There's a BMW ragtop parked out on the street. Maybe that's his."

"Maybe." Fenway turned the man's head slightly to the left. "Are we getting backup any time soon? We need to get this building secured."

"I just spoke to Sheriff Donnelly—twelve-car pile-up just outside of P.Q. Most of the units are on-scene."

Fenway looked up. "And we haven't been called out to that?"

"No fatalities. Not yet, anyway." Dez gestured to the body. "What do you think?"

"Blunt force trauma," Fenway said. "About an inch deep. Looks like a weapon with an unusual shape."

"What kind of unusual shape?"

Fenway pulled out a small flashlight and shined it over the wound. "Well-defined edges. Maybe a cut gemstone—like if the world's biggest engagement ring struck him on the back of the head."

Dez grunted and stood up.

Fenway laid the man's head back on the floor. "What's wrong, Dez?"

Dez crinkled her nose. "I don't mind telling you, this place gives me the creeps."

"More than using an ancient-sounding text so they can justify obstructing an investigation?"

"That's part of it," Dez said, then lowered her voice. "You know the Monument Brotherhood didn't officially let in their first Black member until five years ago."

Fenway blinked. "Only five years ago?"

"And the Central Coast chapter has yet to break the color barrier. Secret societies have their secrets." Dez glanced over at the doorway again. "You should have seen the blond guy who answered the door. He actually called the Sheriff's Office to verify my badge before he'd let me in."

"I guess you warmed him up to me, then."

"It won't surprise you to learn that he voted for Dr. Ivanovich. He volunteered that information when I told him the coroner was on her way."

Fenway nodded, then murmured, "Do you think we should get Mark down here?"

Dez considered, then shook her head. "The Monument Brotherhood is never helpful. I don't think they'll talk to a white sergeant any more than they'll talk to us."

"I don't know a lot about the Monument Brotherhood." Fenway glanced at Dez. "Do you?"

"I've heard stories." Dez stepped closer and lowered her voice. "For years and years, if anyone wanted anything done in Dominguez County, they had to be a member of the Monument Brotherhood. They owned the Sheriff's Office, they owned the banks—if they didn't like you, you couldn't get anywhere."

"So what changed?"

"Nathaniel Ferris," Dez replied. "Your daddy came in and set up his oil company thirty-five years ago, and suddenly the balance of power shifted."

Fenway raised her eyebrows. "How come they didn't recruit him, then?" But as soon as the words were out of her mouth, Fenway knew: it was because he'd married a Black woman. "Okay—but if they didn't want us down here, why did they call the police? Wouldn't it have been easier to move the body, or—I don't know—hide it in the secret catacombs under the building?"

"I can tell you're joking about the catacombs, but I wouldn't put it past them," Dez said thoughtfully. "This is the oldest stone building in Dominguez County—I think it was built in the 1870s. There might be secret passageways below this floor. Hell, for all we know, this could be a trapdoor, and we might fall into a snake pit."

"Just because they're mysterious doesn't make them spy villains from a nineties action movie." Fenway picked the head back up. "Dez, take some pictures of this head wound, would you?"

Dez nodded and pulled out her phone, tapped on the keys, and took a few photos.

"Email them to me?"

Dez tapped again, then swore softly. "No signal."

"Hah. Pretty stereotypical for the headquarters of a secret society."

"Not the headquarters," a deep voice behind them said.

Fenway, startled, flinched—and almost dropped the man's head onto the parquet floor.

"Excuse me," Dez said, "this room is a crime scene."

"I am honored to be the High Worshipful Master of the Monument Brotherhood," the man said. "Redmond Northwall." He had entered the ballroom, but stood twenty feet away from Fenway and Dez.

Fenway appraised Northwall. She'd seen him before: a narrow face with a sharp nose, a full, brown beard and curly hair, with small, piercing gray eyes. He appeared to be in his late forties or early fifties, and, like the dead man on the parquet floor, was dressed in gray trousers, a white dress shirt, and a light purple tie with the initials "MB" embroidered near the bottom.

"You own Radical Familiar Software," Fenway said.

Northwall nodded. "I've been told there's been a—a body found."

"That's correct," Fenway replied. "And I'm the county coroner."

"Yes, Miss Stevenson, I know who you are." He said it with a slight edge to his voice; perhaps *all* the members of the Monument Brotherhood had voted for Dr. Richard Ivanovich for County Coroner.

"Do you know who he is?"

"I'd have to come closer."

Fenway nodded, and Northwall strode to the body in the middle of the floor, glanced down, and frowned.

"Yes," he said, "I know who it is."

Fenway waited a moment, then prodded. "Can you tell us?"

"Frank Mortimer."

"From the way he's dressed," Fenway said, "he'd have been a member of the Monument Brotherhood as well. Is that correct?"

"Yes."

Fenway waited a moment.

Northwall stood, arms at his side, shoulders loose. His face was a blank slate.

"How long has he been a member of the Monument Brotherhood?"

"I don't know." His answer was immediate and curt.

Fenway shifted her weight onto her right knee. "Surely it's in your records."

Northwall was silent.

Fenway sighed. "Mr. Northwall—"

"You didn't ask a question," Northwall said.

Fenway gritted her teeth—was he being purposely unhelpful? "Would you be able to look in your records and give me information about Frank Mortimer?"

"We don't keep records."

No question about it now—he was doing everything he could to block her questions. "If that's how you'd like to play this, Mr. Northwall, I can assure you I can get a subpoena."

"I didn't say I wouldn't show you the records. I said we don't *keep* records. You can get a subpoena all you like, but we can't produce something we don't have."

"If you've destroyed—"

"I take it you are unfamiliar with the workings of the Monument Brotherhood."

"I know people in this town say you're a secret society."

Northwall said nothing and stared straight ahead, his eyes unfocused.

Fenway realized she hadn't asked a question. "Did you know Frank Mortimer?"

"Yes."

"What was he doing here in the ballroom this afternoon?"

"I don't know."

"Does he have any enemies? Anyone who would wish him ill?"

Northwall blinked, then took out a business card from his shirt pocket. "The Monument Brotherhood requires an oath pledging allegiance and secrecy."

Fenway stood and took the card from Northwall's hand. "Lynn Hayes, Esquire," she read. "This your lawyer?"

"The attorney for the Central Coast chapter of the Monument Brotherhood," Northwall said. "If you have any other questions, direct them to Ms. Hayes."

Fenway stood, pointing her finger at Northwall. "If you won't help the investigation, then I suggest you leave the murder scene."

"This is my place of business. I won't—"

"Dez, get him out of here or charge him with interfering with an officer."

Northwall held up his hands. "I'm not here to argue with you, Coroner. I'm simply stating my rights to the property for which I am legally responsible."

Dez moved between Northwall and Fenway. "You heard the coroner. Time to leave the room."

Northwall took a few steps backward, Dez boxing him out of the room like a collie herding sheep into a pen. Northwall gave Fenway a serene smile over Dez's shoulder. "Good luck with your investigation." He turned and began to walk out of the room.

"We're looking for an object with a head shaped like a cut gemstone," Fenway called after him. "Do you have anything like that at this location?"

Northwall slowed his walk for a moment, but he didn't respond as he walked through the doorway and down the hall.

Dez folded her arms as she stared at the empty hallway, then turned back to Fenway. "He spoke at the Nidever University commencement last year. He usually comes off as much more personable."

Fenway walked toward the hallway and peered down the empty corridor. "If he's CEO, that can't be how he addresses his board of directors."

"Then I'll attribute his open hostility to having us sullying the temple with our presence." Dez scratched her nose. "You know, Harrison Walker—your predecessor—was a member here."

Fenway walked back to the body. "From everything I heard about the man, that's no surprise."

"He used to have long lunches with some pretty powerful men in the county," Dez said.

"Like Nathaniel Ferris, I bet."

"Yes—but your daddy wasn't at these lunches. No, the men I'm talking about were from the Monument Brotherhood. I was having lunch at Roxanne's downtown when a few of the members came in. They had a couple of cocktails, and one of them mentioned something called the Bloodstone Scepter. My ears perked up at the term 'blood'—we had a couple of open cases at the time—but then the others shushed him."

"The Bloodstone Scepter?" Fenway rolled her eyes. "Do these secret societies know how stupid this stuff sounds?"

Dez shrugged. "Considering we know nothing about what goes on in this building—and considering that if Mr. Northwall is correct and that they never keep records—this might be all we have to go on. You're looking for a stick or a club with a head that's shaped like a gemstone. Maybe that's the Bloodstone Scepter. I certainly can't think of anything else that would fit the bill."

Fenway nodded. "So, how do we do this?"

"We may have gotten through the front door and into the ballroom," Dez said, "but there are rooms off the hallway that were closed—not to mention another section of the temple."

"We need to get this building searched. If there is such a thing as the Bloodstone Scepter, chances are pretty good that it's here, right?"

"Your guess is as good as mine. But if they use it in ceremonies and important chapter functions, yes, it's probably here." She paused. "Unless..."

"Unless what?"

"If it's the murder weapon, even if it *is* a sacred most worshipful object or whatever, the killer likely took it and disposed of it. Or at least hid it."

"I'll call Melissa and get the CSI team over here right away."

"Do you think he was killed in the ballroom?"

Fenway stared at the floor. "Highly polished wood floor—I'd see drag marks if the body had been moved."

"Unless there were multiple people who carried him."

"Perhaps. But the amount of blood under his head suggests he was killed here." Fenway pointed to a few drops of red about three feet away from his feet. "I think he was standing when he was struck in the head, then fell." She took out her phone and took pictures of the droplets.

"Onto his back, not his stomach? With that hard of a hit?"

"It's not unheard of," Fenway said, but as soon as the words were out of her mouth, she took a breath. "Wait a sec..."

"What?"

"No wallet," Fenway mused. "If he kept his wallet in his front pocket, maybe the killer rolled him onto his back to take his cash and cards."

"Could be." Dez shook her head. "But this can't be a mugging.

Look at this place. And it's five-thirty on a Tuesday evening. They had people here."

"We were joking about the catacombs earlier—but why exactly *did* they call the police?"

"9-1-1 got the call," Dez said. "I assume it was either a member of the brotherhood or someone from the cleaning staff."

"And nobody's talking."

"That's right."

"Okay," Fenway said. "Rigor hasn't set in yet." She knelt next to the scattered blood droplets and touched one gingerly with a gloved finger. "Still slightly wet. He's been dead less than an hour." She looked up. "When did we get the call?"

"Thirty minutes ago."

"Did you interview the cleaning staff?"

"No cleaning staff when I got here. Or at least the three men I spoke with earlier weren't making anyone available." Dez turned the page of her notebook. "All I've got are their names. Chad Wilkenson—he had a mustache and goatee, very well kept. Looked like he was maybe thirty. Benjamin Nichols. He's the blond who didn't believe Black people could be police sergeants."

"He votes," Fenway said dryly.

"And Travis Foxwell. He and Chad could be brothers—I wouldn't have been able to tell them apart without Chad's facial hair."

"Chad, Ben, and Travis. Did the person who called it in give a name?"

"I don't have it. I'll have to track it down."

"I'll call Sarah and see if she can get the name from the 9-1-1 dispatcher."

Dez looked at her watch.

"Oh—right. It's five thirty. Maybe I'll get lucky and she hasn't gone home for the day."

"I'm sure Sarah would love the overtime."

Fenway nodded and tapped her phone. "Oh, of course, no service."

"Thick concrete walls, but I bet they've got some sort of jamming technology."

"Which I'm sure is all *completely* legal," Fenway muttered sarcastically. "All right, I'll go get my fingerprint kit and I'll call Sarah. Then I'll see how quickly CSI can get here from San Miguelito." Fenway pointed to the roll of crime scene tape still in Dez's hand. "Cordon this room off. Then try to get the Monument Brotherhood to open the rest of the building to a search."

"They won't agree."

"We have all kinds of probable cause to search without a warrant," Fenway said.

"Doesn't mean they'll let us in."

"Okay—then let's prepare for the worst. I'll ask Sarah to fill out a warrant application and if the Brotherhood says no, I'll have her call a judge, too," Fenway said. "Sarah was just telling me she needs a new laptop. With the overtime tonight, I'll be her fairy godmother."

CHAPTER TWO

"Sarah, did I catch you before you left the office?" Fenway stepped into the street, expelling the stale air from the temple ballroom from her lungs, her phone pressed to her ear.

"I was just about to lock up."

"What would you say to a little overtime tonight?"

Sarah chuckled. "Exactly how little are we talking about?"

"I need a trace on a call that went into 9-1-1 around five o'clock this afternoon."

"That shouldn't take long."

"We probably need a search for DMV records, too."

"Easy as pie."

"And fill out a warrant application."

"Oh, I see you've saved the best for last." Sarah sighed. "You're just lucky I don't have a date tonight."

"It's Tuesday."

"Which is why you should be at Dos Milagros enjoying your double taco special instead of—wherever you are."

"The Monument Brotherhood Temple on First Street."

"What are you doing there? I didn't think they allowed—"

Silence.

Fenway cleared her throat. "I think it's a little different when one is a law enforcement representative."

"Sure," Sarah said quickly, the sound of a pen scratching on a pad. "I'll trace the 9-1-1 call regarding the Monument Brotherhood. And what about the warrant?"

"It's for searching the Monument Brotherhood Temple."

Sarah sucked in her breath sharply. "That's a can of worms. Are you sure?"

"The dead body has its skull bashed in, Sarah. Evidence of a crime—very clear basis for probable cause. We're about to ask to perform a search of the temple, but Dez thinks they're going to insist on a warrant. So I figured I'd get a head start on it."

"You mean you figured that *I'd* get a head start on it."

"At time-and-a-half."

"Well—yeah." Sarah laughed. "What shall I put in the description?"

"We're searching for the murder weapon: a blunt object with a gemstone-like head."

"Gemstone-like…" Sarah trailed off, then coughed lightly. "That sounds an awful lot like you're asking for the Bloodstone Scepter."

Fenway paused. "How do *you* know about the Bloodstone Scepter?"

"Years ago, the Monument Brotherhood had a chapter in Windkettle. My dad was a member. He had some of his brothers over to the house for meetings after some storm damage to the building. They thought I was in bed."

"Ah."

"Every chapter has a scepter like that."

"Do you know where it's kept?"

"Uh—not really. But I know the High Worshipful Master has

command of the Scepter. So I guess they either keep it under lock and key at the temple or the master keeps it with him. Maybe he takes it home."

"Then perhaps you can fill out a second warrant application for Redmond Northwall's house, too."

"Do you want the whole county to get pissed off at you, Coroner?"

Fenway scoffed. "Surely not everyone in town is associated with the Monument Brotherhood."

"Now that your dad has retired..." Sarah lowered her voice. "Your father came into Estancia before I was born and started Ferris Energy. I've heard stories—the Brotherhood used to run the town. You had to be a member if you wanted to get elected to anything in the county."

"Then my dad changed all that?"

"When you run one of the largest independent oil firms in the country, you don't need ties into the Brotherhood. And that means their influence faded pretty fast. No one needed the brotherhood to get a job at Ferris Energy or to do business with anyone at the company."

Fenway let a long, low whistle. "I had no idea."

"But now that Ferris Energy got sold to Sierra Madre last month, there's a power vacuum. And I think the Brotherhood is trying to take over again. They want the influence in Estancia that they had before Ferris Energy came to town—they've been waiting for this moment for decades."

"Be that as it may," Fenway said, "we've got a dead Brotherhood member at the temple, and we need to find the murder weapon. I don't care if it turns out to be the Holy Grail—if it's at the temple, we have to find it."

"I'll need your signature on the warrant."

"Let me know when it's ready—I'll run over. Do you have everything else you need?"

"Just a couple of questions on the form," Sarah said. "The offense is murder?"

"Homicide. On the form, list out the code sections for both murder and manslaughter. This wasn't an accidental death."

"There's a section on the form to list the facts the application is based on."

"The dead body of Frank Mortimer. And the size and shape of the wound in the back of his skull." Fenway ran a hand over her hair and almost jumped—instead of her usual locks, it was just short, rough fuzz. Her adventure in Los Angeles, when she'd shaved her head, hadn't been more than three weeks ago, but it seemed like a lifetime. She shook her head to clear the memory from her brain.

"Oh—one more thing, Sarah."

Sarah chuckled. "You really want to get your money's worth from my overtime tonight, don't you?"

"See what information you can find on Frank Mortimer. All I know is that he looks like he's in his fifties, and he's a member of the Monument Brotherhood."

"Got anything else to go on? A driver's license with an address, maybe?"

"He didn't have a wallet on him, but he had a BMW key."

"This regarding the DMV search you mentioned earlier?"

"Right. Maybe DMV records will show something useful."

"License plate number?"

"Uh..." Fenway scratched her head. Dez had said the BMW was parked out front. She looked up and down the street. About eight spaces away from the spot directly in front of the building entrance was a silver BMW 328i convertible.

"I think I see the car. Hold on." Fenway walked over to the BMW and read Sarah the license plate number.

"Okay, I'm on it," Sarah said. "I'll call you when the warrant application is ready for a signature."

They said their goodbyes and Fenway tried to peer inside the car. Its side windows were tinted, and she couldn't get a good look. From what she could make out, the front seats were clean, and the car was well-maintained. Not exactly laden with clues, but maybe the trunk or the glove compartment would reveal something.

No matter; Mortimer's keys were in his pocket. Once the CSI team had taken the body to the M.E.'s office in San Miguelito, she could take his keys and search his car—or CSI could do it—before they took the contents of his pockets as evidence.

She turned back to the building—and almost bumped into Dez.

"What are you doing here?"

Dez clenched and unclenched her fists. "I'm locked out."

"Locked out? Of the crime scene?"

"That's right."

"How did that happen?"

"Just after I cordoned off the crime scene, Chad—that's the one with the goatee—asked if he could speak to me outside. I figured he had something important to say if he didn't want to be in the building to do it. So I followed him out the side door, the exit on Guadalupe Avenue—and he tells me the temple is a sacred place, blessed by a bunch of people I'd never heard of, and that an investigation is unwarranted. I told him we'd be as respectful as possible, but this is a murder. He just turned and walked away."

"And they locked you out?"

"That's right. When I went back to the side door, it was locked, and then I went around to the front, and it's locked too. And no one's answering."

Fenway frowned and crossed her arms. "All right. I didn't want to do this, but they're all behaving like hostile witnesses. You said Chad's the one who walked you out?"

"Yes."

"I don't know if we can prove that he colluded with Brad and Tad—"

"Ben and Travis."

"—in locking you out of the building, but we can certainly go after the other two."

"Obstruction?"

"Right. Section 184—and Redmond Northwall too. And I want to scare them when we pull them in. Maximum fine and penalty—I think it might be a full year in jail."

Dez's upper lip curled. "I don't know. I agree with you that they *should* be punished to the full extent of the law, but I'm not sure how likely it is to happen."

"What do you mean?"

"Your father might have done a lot to reduce the influence of the Monument Brotherhood, but it doesn't mean they're gone. Lots of local politicians still belong. Sheriff Donnelly's father, for example."

Fenway turned to look down First Street, her eyes losing focus. "Maybe *that's* why we don't have any deputies here to back us up."

"I don't know if I'd jump to any conclusions." Dez put her hands on her hips. "But I'll concede with any other crime scene, other deputies would have gotten here by now—car crash or not."

"We've got to try to get back in there, Dez." Fenway turned to the building and glared at it. "And if we get stopped, at least we'll have a paper trail."

Dez cocked her head. "I've lived in this town a lot longer than you have. You want to make some very powerful enemies, you keep going down this road."

"Do you have a better idea? You don't want to simply ignore that we have a dead body in that building, do you?"

"Maybe," Dez said, crossing her arms, "we get someone they

know and like and respect to talk with them. Get them to see that we need to get in there and do this properly."

"Who are you thinking? Sheriff Donnelly? See if she can talk to her father?"

Dez bit her lip. "I'm not sure she'd come down on our side on this. Gretchen's great, don't get me wrong, but confronting her father—that's a lot of political capital to spend. Besides, Gretchen's the wrong gender."

"Oh. Right. The good ol' boys' club."

Dez tapped her foot on the sidewalk. "I think it might be a good idea to get someone who can speak their language."

"A white male, you mean. Sergeant Trevino?"

Dez shook her head. "Nope. Now, he might not be sheriff anymore, but your boyfriend—"

"McVie? You want McVie to talk to the Monument Brotherhood?"

"That's right."

"We were just talking about how they wouldn't even invite my rich father to join because he was married to a Black woman. If you haven't noticed, Dez, McVie is dating a Black woman, too."

"It's different. They already accept him. He had to talk with them on several cases over the years when he was sheriff. He's one of the few law enforcement people they *would* talk to. And unlike Mark, he knows their language. He knows how to persuade them."

Fenway frowned. "I don't like it."

"You don't have to like it. But I think it's our best bet."

Fenway pointed at Dez. "Then you call him. I don't want him thinking I'm playing the girlfriend card with this one."

Dez laughed. "Playing the girlfriend card? Come on. Play the *county coroner* card. Giving him the opportunity as a P.I. to assist the sheriff's office? We'll owe him access on a future case—and he'll jump at the chance to get it."

Fenway nodded. Dez was right—Fenway needed to lead the investigation. "Let me give these bros one more chance to do this the right way." She strode up the sidewalk to the entrance of the Monument Brotherhood Temple, then pulled on the heavy wooden door: locked. She searched for a bell—there was none. Fenway looked back at Dez, who gave a slight shrug of her shoulders.

Fenway rapped on the door with her knuckles, barely making a sound, the heavy door solid and unmoving.

"Open up, Mr. Northwall. Police!"

Silence. The street in front of the temple was eerily quiet, too. Fenway knocked again—the same weak rapping sound.

"Mr. Northwall! You're obstructing a police investigation!"

Still nothing. She waited a moment, then pulled out her phone and called McVie.

It went to voicemail.

"Craig, call me back. I've got a—a bit of a situation here. Might need your, uh, input."

Fenway hung up. She hated how nervous she sounded on the message. She shook her head to clear her mind, then called Sarah.

"Something else?" Sarah asked when she answered.

"Change the warrant application for Dez, not me. She's on her way to sign it."

"Yeah, I figured the Monument Brotherhood would insist on a warrant."

"They didn't even mention a warrant—they locked us out of the temple."

"What? Weren't the deputies there securing the scene?"

"No." Fenway thought for a moment. "Call Judge Harada and ask her to sign it."

"Judge Harada? I don't think I know her."

"She was just appointed—I think she moved here from the Bay

Area. If there's any judge who doesn't have a history with the Monument Brotherhood, it's her."

"Makes sense. I should have it ready in a few minutes."

"Thanks." Fenway hesitated. "And in addition to the search warrant for Redmond Northwall, add an arrest warrant, too."

"For Redmond? Are you sure?"

"He's obstructing an investigation. Penal code section 148."

"I don't think that's a good idea, Fenway."

"We can talk about it later—I'd rather have it and not need it than need it and not have it."

"Okay. I'll add it to the list."

Fenway ended the call, then she turned and walked to Dez. "Head back to the office. Sarah's filling out a few warrant applications and they need your signature."

"A few?"

"A search warrant for the temple, one for Northwall's house, and an arrest warrant for Northwall."

"Is that a good idea?" Dez pursed her lips. "Arresting a software CEO who's also the leader of—"

"He's keeping us from a dead body, Dez. Just because he's a special snowflake doesn't mean he gets a free pass to keep us from investigating a murder."

"I'm not saying he gets a pass. Just that there might be a better way."

Fenway looked up at Dez. "I'm open to better ways. I don't want this to get political any more than you do."

Dez was silent.

"Well," Fenway said, "maybe we'll think of something. Even if we get the warrant, it doesn't mean we have to use it."

Dez motioned to the temple with her head. "You sure you don't want me to stay here, make sure no one leaves? Someone might abscond with the murder weapon."

"You can't cover all the exits—whoever's in there might have already left when Chad came out and talked to me. And we've left the exits unattended for so long, the killer may be gone by now." Fenway thought for a moment. "In fact, maybe I should see if Redmond Northwall has gone home."

"Probably worth checking out."

"On your way to the office, call dispatch again—see if they can spare anyone from the crash in P.Q. to come here." Fenway scratched her head; her hair prickled her palm. "And call Deputy Salvador. If she's available, have her look up the Northwalls' address and tell her to meet me there."

CHAPTER THREE

Fenway parked her Accord next to the curb under a streetlight, its bright glow casting harsh shadows on the quiet residential street. She looked across the road to the large house, its tall arches framing the well-lit doorway. To the left and slightly behind the front of the main house, a four-car garage—with similar arches and other architectural details—stood behind a row of tall Italian cypresses.

A police cruiser pulled up behind Fenway and turned its engine and lights off. Fenway got out of the Honda to greet Deputy Celeste Salvador as she emerged from her vehicle.

Deputy Salvador was a few inches shorter than Fenway, in her early thirties. Her shoulder-length dark hair was pulled back into a ponytail. She looked at Fenway with wary dark brown eyes. "Do we think the suspect is here?"

"Redmond Northwall. I don't know—I'm applying for a warrant for obstruction at the very least."

"Think it'll come through?"

"Sarah's pulled off miracles before." Fenway shuffled her feet on the asphalt. "If he's the killer, I'm sure he would know that we'd look for him here. So my money is that he's back at the temple or in the wind. If he's here, either he's supremely confident in his ability to trick us, or he's innocent."

"This guy is the CEO of a software company, right? A successful one?"

"That's right."

"Did you read that study that said CEOs are ten times more likely to be sociopaths than the overall population?"

"I did."

"No offense to your dad."

Fenway chuckled. "None taken."

Celeste motioned toward the house. "Did you put out an APB on his car?"

"Not yet. I want to see if he's here."

Celeste motioned to the house with her chin. "It's well lit. Looks like *someone's* home, anyway."

Fenway took a deep breath. "You ready?"

"Let's do it."

They crossed the road and walked up the stone footpath to the front door, a reddish-tinged mahogany with ornate glass windows. Fenway reached out and touched the bell; Westminster chimes rang from inside.

A moment later, a woman opened the door. Trim and athletic, she wore a black business suit with a brooch in the shape of a dolphin on the lapel. Her red hair cascaded down past her shoulders, and she had freckles across the pale skin of her cheeks and nose. She was likely in her early forties, without the treatments and plastic surgeries that Fenway halfway expected from a famous CEO's wife. She smiled easily. "Yes?"

"County Coroner Fenway Stevenson." Fenway held her identification out.

The woman peered at it, her smile faltering.

"This is my colleague, Deputy Celeste Salvador. Is this the residence of Redmond Northwall?"

"Yes." The woman stepped out onto the front step, closing the door behind her and crossing her arms. "What can I help you with?"

"Do you live here as well?"

"Yes. I'm Emma Northwall, Red's wife. What's this about?"

"We need to speak with your husband. Is he home?"

"No. I believe he had a business dinner." She paused. "Speaking of which, I've got a dinner to get to myself."

"This will only take a moment, Mrs. Northwall. When was the last time you saw him?"

"About twenty minutes ago."

"Twenty minutes ago?"

"Yes." Emma pointed back at the house. "He came home from work, ran in the house, said hi to me, then said he had to go out again, and went to the garage."

"The garage?"

"Of course. He drove his car home and took it back out."

"He parked it in the garage, then drove it back out?"

"That's what I just said." Emma crinkled her nose.

"What kind of car?"

"A Tesla Model S—what did you say this was about?"

"He's the leader of the local chapter of the Monument Brotherhood, is he not?"

"Uh—that's correct. I'm pretty sure that's a matter of public record."

"How long did he spend in the garage?"

"Only about fifteen—" Emma paused, then looked from Fenway's face to Celeste's and back again. "California has a policy of spousal privilege," she said carefully.

Fenway was silent. This wasn't good.

"You can't compel me to give information against my husband," Emma continued.

"Testimony," Celeste said.

"What?" Emma asked.

Fenway winced, then glanced at Celeste. "Testimony, not information. But we're not accusing your husband of anything."

Emma folded her arms. "What is this information regarding?"

"There was an incident at the temple this evening and we wanted to ask him if he could give us any details."

"An incident?"

"That's right," Fenway said. When she started as coroner last year, she might have spilled the beans about the murder, but that would definitely shut Emma down. It might not make much difference in this case—Emma looked like she didn't trust Fenway anyway. "I wonder," she said as calmly as she could, "if he left the information we need in the garage. If we could just—"

"I think it's time for you two to leave," Emma Northwall said. "I'll fully cooperate with warrants and subpoenas, but I have nothing else to say at this time, and I decline to allow you to search anything on my property."

"Fair enough," Fenway said. "Have a good night."

Fenway turned and walked back down the stone pathway to the street, Celeste on her heels.

"Sorry," Celeste mumbled.

"For what?"

"I said one word, and it's the word that shut her down."

Fenway shrugged. "She was getting suspicious of us anyway. I wouldn't have been able to search the garage no matter what you'd said."

They walked across the street to their cars.

"Not what I expected," Fenway said.

"What?"

"Emma Northwall. She's not that much younger than Redmond. I was expecting a trophy wife with plastic surgery."

Celeste glanced back at the house. "The *Courier* did a piece on her charity a few weeks ago. Some save-the-ocean thing. She's got a degree in marine biology—she's no one's trophy." She frowned as she approached the police cruiser. "But I got the feeling she's hiding something. She knows—or at least strongly suspects—what her husband might have hidden in the garage."

"I agree," Fenway said. "I've already got Sarah filling out a warrant application for this house."

"Does that include the garage?"

"Sarah's done this before," Fenway said, evading the question, but made a mental note to check with her. "And Dez is signing the warrants. So I'm sure it'll be okay."

"And you caught what she said, right?" Celeste asked. "He was in the garage for 'fifteen'—something. Probably minutes."

Fenway nodded. "And he pulled all the way into the garage. If you know you're just running in the house to get something, you don't drive into the garage. You park in the driveway. In a neighborhood like this, you probably don't even lock your car."

"Unless you need to hide a murder weapon." Celeste unlocked the cruiser. "You *would* pull in the garage all the way. You don't want your neighbors seeing your bloody baseball bat."

"Bloodstone scepter."

"Bloodstone scepter," Celeste muttered. "Seriously?"

"It's cosplay for white men," Fenway said.

"Yeah." Celeste opened the door of the cruiser. "It's all fun and games until one of them gets their brains bashed in."

"And then it's just fun."

Celeste didn't even chuckle, her brow creased in thought.

"You ever think about taking the detective exam?"

Celeste looked up. "Scheduled for April."

———

As Celeste drove away in the cruiser, Fenway got back into her Accord. She pulled out her phone and sent a message to Sarah to include the garage in the warrant, then remembered that she hadn't gotten a call back from McVie. Especially with Redmond North-well going in and out of his garage—and with his scepter as a possible murder weapon—she needed someone who could get through to the Monument Brotherhood. She turned the engine on, waiting for the phone to connect to Bluetooth, and tapped the screen.

Two rings. "McVie Investigations," a high-pitched woman's voice said.

"Has Craig got you working late again, Piper?"

"Hello to you too." Piper chuckled. "Don't worry about me. I'm taking comp time—a long weekend with Migs since he passed the bar. Can you believe he's never been to the Grand Canyon?"

"Yeah, well, I've never been either."

Piper gasped. "Never?"

"Not all of us—" Fenway paused. Maybe she *had* gone to the Grand Canyon, back when her parents were still together, and she just didn't remember. "Never mind. Can you put him on?"

"Sure."

A moment later: "Hey, Fenway. I might have some client work tonight—I'm not sure when I can get away."

"Oh, right." Vaguely, Fenway remembered they'd made dinner plans—or plans to make plans, anyway. "I'm caught up in a case myself. And I thought you could help me."

"Help you?"

"I heard that when you were sheriff, you used to run into the Monument Brotherhood."

Silence on the other end.

"Craig?"

"I'm here. I—" McVie drew in his breath sharply. "They don't have the power they used to, but they still have control of a lot of stuff in Estancia."

"Like what?"

"Maybe *control* is the wrong word. Let's try *influence*. Like the hiring practices at a lot of local places—the ones your dad didn't own, anyway. A couple of the county agencies, too. They finally got voted out of the school board about a decade ago—anyway, that's in the past. Do you need me to connect you with one of the members?"

"I need to figure out how to get our CSI team into the temple."

McVie hesitated. "That's a tall order. You better have an unimpeachable reason for wanting—"

"A dead body on the floor of their ballroom."

Silence.

"You there, Craig?"

"This is tough. There are a few judges in the county who are still members of the Brotherhood. Benson, Haggarty, Pressway."

"Then they should recuse themselves."

"But you know they won't."

"I'm having Judge Harada sign the search warrant, but I hope it won't come to that."

"Are you asking me to contact them and—do what, exactly?"

"Sweet-talk them? Pal around with them, tell them we're not so bad?"

"I don't think I hold the sway over them you think I do."

"Not me—Dez thought you'd be the right person to talk with them."

"Oh. Well, I'm glad I made such a good impression on her, but I can't…" His voice trailed off.

"What is it?"

"I, uh, I've swept some things under the rug for them. It's not something I'm proud of."

Fenway blinked. "Why—why would you do that?"

"Because they run a lot of this town. Like a restaurant suddenly gets its liquor license pulled because the owner fired the son of one of the Brotherhood members. Stuff like that." He stumbled over his words. "So, so, uh—I pulled some strings, and they pulled some strings."

"Ah."

"I'll call my contacts if you want, but now that I'm not sheriff, I can't convince them to do much of anything."

"I see."

"I've—uh, I've also got a client who is involved with the Monument Brotherhood. It's an ethical conflict of interest. Maybe. Was the dead person involved with the brotherhood?"

Fenway hesitated for a moment—it wasn't public knowledge, but McVie was trustworthy. "Frank Mortimer."

McVie sighed heavily. "You think it was foul play?"

"Absolutely."

"Well, that's not good. It's not good at all. You better come down here. I've got a ton of information that'll be pertinent to your investigation."

Fenway's stomach growled. She looked at the clock: it was past six-thirty. She put the Accord into Drive, turned the car around, and drove toward downtown.

CHAPTER FOUR

Fenway dropped a small, heavy paper bag on McVie's desk.

"What's this?"

"Figured the least I could do for you is buy you and Piper dinner."

"This isn't your way of tricking me into eating lengua, is it?"

"Carnitas burrito, extra tomatillo salsa." Fenway set the drink carrier down and pulled a soda out and set it next to the bag.

"This wasn't really what I had in mind when I asked you to dinner tonight."

Fenway shrugged. "It's the job. And it's a Tuesday."

McVie reached into the bag. "I can give you *some* details of my investigation—the parts that are relevant to Frank Mortimer. Beyond that, I can't provide any identifying information."

Fenway nodded. "Anything you have that's considered attorney work product is off the table, right?"

McVie pulled the foil-wrapped burrito out and set it on his desk. "Fortunately for you, I haven't gotten involved with the lawyers yet. " He raised his head. "Piper, would you bring in the Emma Northwall file?"

"Emma Northwall?" Fenway asked. "I just talked to her. This must be one of your cheating-spouse cases."

A willowy redhead appeared in the doorway to McVie's office, a folder squeezed between her elbow and her side.

Fenway handed Piper another burrito from the bag.

Piper took it. "You're not eating?"

Fenway felt the color rise to her cheeks. "I ate my tacos in the car on the way over." And spilled some salsa on her trousers. She took the folder from Piper and set it on McVie's desk. "So, what am I looking at, Craig?"

"Six weeks ago, Emma Northwall hired me to determine whether her husband was having an affair."

Piper looked up at Fenway as she unwrapped the top of her burrito. "He's the CEO of Radical Familiar."

Fenway nodded. "Emma seemed like she was going to a business dinner tonight."

"She's on the board of a charity—Dominguez Ocean Rescue. They have a fundraising dinner tonight." Piper took a big bite of her burrito.

"Nice to have a client who works for good."

Piper swallowed, then pulled the foil farther down on her burrito. "She told us her husband—Redmond Northwall—was acting strangely. Staying at the office much later than usual, saying he'd gone on a business trip, and when she called the office, he'd taken a sick day instead." She took another bite.

"Classic signs." McVie wiped his hand on a paper napkin. "Emma had taken a couple of pictures on her phone of Redmond Northwall and a young woman that Emma didn't recognize. Seemed to be in her early twenties."

Piper pointed with her pinkie, her mouth full. "Open the folder."

The folder contained a stack of pages and photos; on top, a photo of a young white woman with strawberry-blonde hair, high cheekbones, full lips, large hazel eyes.

"Haley Sinclair," Piper said. "Grad student at Nidever University, getting her masters in computer science."

The next page was an array of smaller photos, all of Haley Sinclair in various superhero outfits. Several taken at conventions with what looked like rabid fans, and a few of her in a revealing Jewels of Carthage costume at a tradeshow booth with the Radical Familiar Software logo above a computer station.

"Full-time student, part-time cosplayer," Piper said. "I'm still doing research on her—she's got a lot of tangled-up social media accounts."

"Her costumes are good."

"I hear she has a designer, but that might just be from other envious cosplayers."

Fenway pointed to the tradeshow photo. "That's the company that Redmond Northwall owns."

"The CEO," Piper corrected. "Sold controlling interest to a private equity firm a few years ago, but otherwise, yes."

"So he's sleeping with Haley Sinclair? She's got to be less than half his age."

"Not that simple," McVie said through a bite of burrito. He used his free hand to turn to the next page. A hotel bill from the Phillips-Holsen.

Fenway squinted. "Frank Mortimer—this is his bill?"

"That's right." McVie turned the page again, this time to another array of photos.

The first photo showed a Tesla Model S in the parking structure of the Phillips-Holsen. The second photo was the same Tesla, but with the photo enhanced. Haley Sinclair's face could clearly be seen through the passenger window.

"Does this Tesla belong to Redmond Northwall?"

"It does," Piper said.

The second photo showed Haley Sinclair, in a short white dress and strappy sandals—a much different look than her super-hero outfits. She was frozen in mid-stride, walking confidently through the lobby of the Phillips-Holsen. The third photo showed her embracing a man, an inch or two taller than Sinclair. The man was white, late fifties, bald and clean-shaven, with a thin face and pointed features, a black leather laptop bag over his shoulder.

"That's Frank Mortimer," Fenway said.

"Right." Piper pinkie-pointed at the fourth photograph. "That's the two of them getting into the elevator, and that is definitely his hand on her ass."

"You're getting good with the camera, Piper."

McVie cleared his throat. "I took those pictures."

"Ah—you were already good." Fenway smiled at McVie, then furrowed her brow. "I'm not following. Redmond Northwall chauffeurs a hired cosplayer to a hotel for one of his Monument Brothers to hook up with?"

"Didn't make a lot of sense to us, either," McVie said. "So we started digging into the financials."

This time, it was Piper's turn to clear her throat.

"And by *we*, I mean Piper," McVie said, then took another bite of his burrito.

"Starting in November," Piper said, "Haley Sinclair has been getting weekly checks from Radical Familiar for a thousand dollars. Then three weeks ago—in fact, the day after this photo was taken—she gets a check for seventy-five hundred."

Fenway pinched the bridge of her nose. "The company paid a

grad student to have sex with one of the CEO's secret society brothers."

"That's what we thought at first, too," McVie said. "Then Piper suggested we look into both the company financials and into Frank Mortimer's finances."

"But—Piper, you just said Radical Familiar is backed by a private equity firm. Those numbers aren't public."

Piper shrugged. "There are people who will share those numbers with you if you ask them the right way."

"I don't think I want to hear about this," Fenway said. "And if you didn't obtain these legally, I can't use any of this in court."

"What I *can* say," Piper said, "is that Frank Mortimer celebrated his thirtieth wedding anniversary last month. And I can also say that he's the chief financial officer of Radical Familiar."

"Redmond Northwall didn't mention that at the temple. The CEO is paying for his own CFO to sleep with—" Fenway's eyes went wide. "Is this setup for blackmail? Trying to force Frank Mortimer out?"

"Or it could be some weird sex thing with the Monument Brotherhood," Piper said.

"Those are both possibilities," McVie said.

"But we haven't been right about anything yet," Piper said. "I'm still digging. Mortimer's made some big withdrawals from his 401(k). I'm trying to figure out where that money went."

"Maybe paying off the blackmailer," Fenway suggested.

Piper shook her head. "This happened months ago. Not just his 401(k)—Mortimer liquidated some of his other assets, too. Sold some land he had up in Humboldt county."

"So suddenly a bunch of money is freed up from his monthly expenses." Fenway shook her head. "And you suspect the blackmailer is the CEO of one of the biggest software firms south of Silicon Valley?"

"That doesn't make a lot of sense," McVie admitted. "Northwall earns millions of dollars a year, plus the private equity firm paid him millions more when he sold the company. Why would he resort to blackmail?"

"Gambling problem?" Fenway mused.

Piper shook her head again. "There's no sign of that."

"What do you think, then?"

Piper grinned. "I think it's the thrill."

"I'm sorry—the thrill?"

"Think about it, Fenway. The guy's done everything he can with money. Started a business from scratch, sold it for hundreds of millions, gets an eight-figure salary. He can take vacations anywhere he wants, he can buy any car he wants. What's left?"

"So you're saying he's blackmailing his own CFO—his own secret society brother—because he's bored?"

Piper bit her lip. "When you put it like that, it doesn't seem so feasible, but that's the only thing that makes sense to me."

"This was three weeks ago—when Mortimer visited the Phillips-Holsen with Haley Sinclair. Any sign of blackmail payments?"

"No. Although if Northwall is doing it just for the thrill, it could be he's just keeping the cash. Maybe putting it in a safe deposit box or putting it in the top drawer of his desk at work."

Fenway crossed her arms. "So now Frank Mortimer is dead on the floor of the ballroom of the Monument Brotherhood Temple. Explain that."

"Confrontation with his blackmailer that got heated," McVie said. "Northwall kills him. I don't know how he died—gunshot? Stabbing?"

"I suppose it could have happened like that," Fenway admitted. "But why target the CFO? Frank and Redmond were secret society brothers. Isn't there supposed to be some sort of bond?"

"People break bonds all the time," Piper said.

Fenway frowned. "That might explain why Redmond killed Frank. But it doesn't explain why Chad, Brad, and Tad are covering for him."

McVie furrowed his brow. "Chad…"

"Sorry—the three other people who were at the temple. They're all covering up for Redmond Northwall."

"I believe it," Piper said. "Bros before—uh, something."

"I don't," McVie said. "Even if Redmond Northwall *is* the High Worshipful Master. Honesty, especially in finances, is highly valued. No one in the Monument Brotherhood would let anyone get away with the murder of one of their own, especially if the killer had been blackmailing the victim."

"Then why are they obstructing our investigation?" Fenway asked. Then she blinked. "What if…"

"What?"

"What if Frank Mortimer is stealing money from Radical Familiar?"

McVie tilted his head. "What makes you think that?"

"Because he's pulling all his money out of his current life," Fenway said, and thought briefly about her mother stealing her away to Seattle. "He doesn't intend on retiring with his wife up north in the redwoods. He's amassing all the capital he has—and I bet he's getting some more."

"That's a leap, Fenway." Piper shook her head. "Even if he *was* thinking of leaving his wife, that doesn't mean he's stealing from the company. Besides, I haven't found any international deposits yet. Not in the Cayman Islands, not in the Bahamas, not in any of those Caribbean shell companies."

"Then where is all that money going? He's not carrying around suitcases of cash, right?"

"No, but—" Piper frowned. "I've been focusing on the

Caribbean, but there are more countries I can look at. Maybe Central America."

McVie took the last bite of his burrito and chewed thoughtfully. "While Piper's researching where Frank Mortimer's money went, I'll make some calls. I know a few people who are still involved. See what they know. Maybe they've heard something."

"You think they'll share it with you?"

"Probably not. But I can ask."

When Fenway drove her Honda onto First Street toward the Monument Brotherhood Temple, several cruisers, their red-and-blue lights spinning, were parked at a variety of angles, one police car even up on the sidewalk next to the door.

She parked a block away, then hurried across the street. Dez stood in front of the door, a bullhorn in her hand, several deputies flanking her. As Fenway approached, Dez raised the bullhorn with a snap of static and a squeak of feedback.

"This is the Dominguez County Sheriff's Office," Dez said, the electronic bullhorn amplifying Dez's voice. Fenway blinked. They all had Kevlar vests on.

Behind her, a deputy hoisted a battering ram into his arms.

"We have a warrant to search the premises," Dez continued. "If you are inside, open the door, raise your hands above your head, and allow our deputies inside."

The building stayed silent.

After a moment, Fenway hurried over to Dez.

"I take it you got the warrant."

"Pretty cut and dried for Judge Harada. Dead body inside, we're locked out. Easy call."

"What about the arrest warrant for Northwall?"

"Harada said we were looking to get in the building. She thought the arrest warrant was—how did she put it?—an 'unnecessary scare tactic.'"

"Maybe someone mentioned how powerful the Brotherhood used to be in the county."

"That was me. I thought she should know what she's getting herself into. We've got another deputy stationed at her house tonight, just in case." Dez raised the bullhorn to her mouth again. "Repeat, we have a warrant to search the premises. If you do not open the door, we will break it down."

Fenway thought back to watching Dez break open the door of a warehouse several months before. Unlike that door, however, these doors were significantly thicker and more secure. "Think the battering ram is strong enough?"

Dez glanced over her shoulder at the deputy holding the battering ram. "I'm not sure," she said. "A door is only as good as its lock, though, and this lock is against a second door, not against a doorframe. There are a few other doors around the back and the sides we can try if this doesn't work. We'll see what we see."

Fenway had a moment of panic—she had forgotten to ask Dez to make sure the warrant for the Northwalls' home included the garage. "Is another team at Redmond Northwall's house?"

"No. Judge Harada was reluctant to issue a warrant for his house. Said there wasn't enough evidence to reasonably assume the murder weapon was in any specific location except the temple. Said we could come back if we didn't find it here, though."

Fenway crinkled her nose. "I didn't tell you and Sarah about my interview with Emma Northwall."

"Oh, that's right—I didn't even ask how that went."

"She told me that Redmond had been home just after we spoke with him. He went in the garage for about fifteen minutes and then left again."

Dez's eyes went wide. "That sounds like just enough time to find a hiding place for a murder weapon."

"That's what I thought too. But then Emma declined to allow me to search. Since we're getting search warrants for both here and the Northwalls' house, we'll find some evidence soon enough."

"Do you think Emma Northwall is hiding something?"

Fenway crossed her arms and stared down at the floor in thought. "She was on her way out the door—Piper said it was some charity fundraiser."

"Oh, right, the Dominguez Ocean Rescue." Dez scratched her head. "If the Bloodstone Scepter isn't here, we'll go back and ask Judge Harada again. This time with the information from your interview."

Fenway motioned with her head to the front door. "You going to break it down?"

"Yep." Dez lifted the bullhorn. "This is your last warning. We have a warrant to search the premises. Stand clear of the doors."

Dez handed the bullhorn to Fenway, and the deputy behind Dez handed her the battering ram. Four other deputies, all in Kevlar vests, fanned out in a half-circle on the sidewalk behind Dez. Vaguely, Fenway remembered McVie saying that Dez was the best on the staff with a battering ram.

Dez walked up to the tall, thick double doors, then turned her body slightly to the side. With a hand on each of the two handles, she swung it back just in front of her hips, and drove the ram where the two doors met, next to the lock—hard.

A thud—higher-pitched than Fenway was expecting.

Dez grimaced. "This door is solid."

She swung the battering ram again, back and forth, back and forth, then drove the ram into the door in the exact same place.

The squealing of tires around the corner. Fenway jerked her head around. An Acura TSX braked hard just in front of a cruiser.

The deputies all turned toward the Acura, with their hands on their holsters.

"Injunction!" a woman's voice yelled from inside the car—its driver's window was down. A piece of paper appeared out of the window.

"Injunction?" Fenway murmured.

"Shit," Dez said, lowering the battering ram to rest against her hips.

"Lynn Hayes, attorney for the Monument Brotherhood. I've got an order for an injunction signed by the honorable Michael J. Haggarty. You must stop breaking into the temple."

Fenway strode over to the car, approaching the driver's side, and looked at the woman. She was in a brown business suit with a cream-colored blouse. Her pale face was flushed red and her dark hair was tousled.

Lynn Hayes handed the document to Fenway. She scanned it—but it looked legitimate. Michael F. Haggarty's signature decorated the bottom.

Fenway looked at the deputies, warily holding their hands over their gun handles. She locked eyes with Dez and shook her head. "Stand down."

CHAPTER FIVE

"This is bullshit," Fenway said, holding the door to the coroner's suite open for Dez.

"I told you they had a lot of influence," Dez said.

Sarah stood from behind the desk. "What happened?"

"Judge Haggarty," Fenway said. "He's a member of the Monument Brotherhood—at least, according to Craig. And he's the one who signed the injunction."

"So you need something else," Sarah said.

"I don't think Judge Haggarty will let *anyone* in there, no matter the evidence," Fenway said. "If a dead body lying in the middle of the ballroom floor won't do it, nothing will."

"The injunction won't stand up to a court challenge," Dez said, "but even if we get the injunction lifted tomorrow morning, that gives the Monument Brotherhood more than twelve hours to remove the body and clean everything up."

"We're still watching the doors," Fenway said.

"And I'm telling you, they've got tunnels and underground caves and secret ancient passageways," Dez said.

"And a Batmobile?" asked Fenway.

Dez ignored her. "We'll go in there tomorrow and the ballroom floor will be so clean you could eat off it. I'll bet you a hundred bucks there'll be no sign of the body."

Fenway folded her arms. "This isn't right."

"And what do you propose we do?" Dez said. "We don't even have a corpse."

Fenway nodded. "Maybe not, but we might not need the actual body. I've got my notes from my initial assessment. Then if I add what happened tonight into the record, a D.A. might decide that's good enough for a murder indictment."

"You do remember there are Monument Brotherhood members all throughout the county administration," Dez said. "Your predecessor was a member. If you don't think this'll be an uphill battle, you're deluding yourself."

"It's a battle I'm willing to fight." Fenway opened the door to her office and put her laptop bag on the desk. She turned to Sarah. "I didn't expect you to still be here."

"I was researching Frank Mortimer. Lots of stuff doesn't fit."

"Yeah—McVie had some information about Frank Mortimer, too."

"McVie had information about our decedent?"

"He took on Redmond Northwall's wife as a client." Fenway relayed the information about the Northwalls, about Haley Sinclair, and about Frank Mortimer.

Sarah nodded thoughtfully. "I agree," she said slowly, "Redmond Northwall as a blackmailer doesn't make much sense. But I think Frank Mortimer was preparing to do something big."

"Something big?"

Sarah reached down and clicked on a browser window. "Here's an online ad for his BMW. He's withdrawn almost everything in his

401(k), in his savings accounts, and his main checking account is down to less than a thousand dollars."

"McVie knew about the 401(k), but this is the first I've heard of his bank accounts."

"He's also stopped his direct deposit from his job—he's been getting paper checks for the last month. He's taken his own name off the credit cards he used to share with his wife, too. I'm applying for a warrant to see if he's current on his mortgage, but I bet he hasn't paid in a few months. His wife will be in for quite a shock."

"Where's it all going?"

"My guess is an account in the Caymans, or something equally hard-to-track. We can only get so far requesting the financial information of murder victims."

Fenway nodded. Piper might be able to track this using other means—though whether Fenway could use that information was debatable. She hoped Piper had found the deposits when she expanded her search to Central America. "Did he put his notice in at work?"

"Not that I've seen."

"Travel plans?"

"I was just about to check the major airlines."

Fenway turned to Dez. "Any ideas about what he might have been doing?"

"Besides leaving his wife?" Dez shrugged. "Not the first time I've heard of a spouse uprooting their whole life and moving halfway around the world. It might be a shitty thing to do, but it's not illegal."

Fenway chuckled. "You know, the first thing I thought of is that he was stealing from his job, but I could be overthinking it. Maybe his wife caught on to what he was doing and killed him herself."

"Yeah, that leapt to mind. I checked, though—she's in Sedona at a spa retreat. Left on Saturday, doesn't get back for two weeks. The instructor said twenty people saw her in yoga class at the time her husband was killed. Poor woman—I bet she has no idea Mortimer had liquidated their assets."

Sarah tilted her head. "Why would you think he's stealing from the company?"

Fenway laced her fingers behind her head and exhaled. "He steals from his wife like that, he won't have a problem stealing from his company either. And I can't think of another scenario that would explain why Redmond Northwall would drop off Haley Sinclair at a five-star hotel to sleep with his CFO. Northwall must have been trying to trap Mortimer for *something.*"

"So—hold on," Sarah said. "You're saying that Sinclair is reporting back to Northwall? Information about his hidden bank accounts, maybe the location he's thinking of going?"

"Well—I'm not sure I thought it through *that* much. But—I suppose it's possible."

Dez scratched her chin. "How much did you say Haley Sinclair received after the night in the hotel?"

"Uh—I don't remember."

"Would Piper know?"

Fenway took out her phone and tapped the screen.

Piper picked up on the second ring. "Hey, Fenway."

"Quick question," Fenway said. "How much did Haley Sinclair receive the night after she stayed in the hotel with Frank Mortimer?"

"You mean on top of those weekly thousand-dollar payments? Online transfer for seventy-five hundred."

"Thanks, Piper. I'll let you get back."

"Before you go—there's something weird going on with Haley. I've been trying to trace her online activity and I keep running into dead ends."

Fenway stared at the ceiling for a moment, thinking. "You think someone at Radical Familiar is covering up her tracks? Maybe all her interactions with Redmond Northwall?"

Piper clicked her tongue. "It's possible. But if it were someone at Radical Familiar, wouldn't their motive be to hide all the shady stuff Northwall is doing—not the shady stuff Haley's doing? Anyway, I'm still digging. I'll let you know what I find." She said her goodbyes and ended the call.

"Well?" Dez asked. "Haley's payment?"

"Oh—seventy-five hundred dollars. On top of the grand she got every week."

"That makes sense," Dez mused. "A relatively small payment to Haley in order to stop Frank from getting away with a huge amount of money. We could be talking about eight figures here. Insider trading—or maybe even straight-up embezzlement. These privately held firms don't have the oversight that public companies do."

"Right." Fenway turned to Sarah. "We find that secret bank account, we'll find motive for murder."

"Not just Redmond Northwall, either," Dez said. "All the investors in the private equity firm. They may have had millions stolen from their personal investments."

Fenway put a hand to her forehead. "Judge Harada."

"What?"

"Judge Harada—she signed the search warrant for the temple."

"Right..." Sarah said.

"How do you think she'd feel if she found out that a member of the Monument Brotherhood just blocked her warrant?"

"I would imagine she wouldn't feel great about it."

"And I can't believe I didn't mention this, Sarah, but Emma Northwall just told us her husband had come home after we spoke to him at the temple. He drove into his garage, then left again—after fifteen minutes."

"She said all that? I can use that in the new warrant application.

That will provide better probable cause." Sarah turned toward the computer and brought up the warrant application in another window. "I'll let you know when it's ready for your signature."

The phone in Fenway's office rang.

"Who's calling you at eight o'clock on a Tuesday night?"

"Someone who knows I'm still working," Fenway said. She hurried into her office and picked up the phone. "Fenway Stevenson."

"Fenway, it's Celeste."

"Hi, Celeste. Did you think of something else regarding Emma Northwall's statement?"

"It's not that. I have three people wanting to make statements concerning the death of Frank Mortimer."

"Three people?"

"Yeah." A shuffling of papers. "Chad Wilkenson, Benjamin Nichols, and Travis Foxwell. All dressed identically in gray pants, white dress shirts, and lavender ties."

Right—the three men Fenway remembered as Chad, Brad, and Tad. "Anyone interviewing them yet?"

"They specifically asked for you."

Fenway pinched the bridge of her nose. "I guess I better come over."

———

Dez had said Chad Wilkenson looked about thirty years old, but Fenway had him pegged for closer to twenty-five. He had a neat, trimmed mustache and goatee, but his hair was fuzzy, as if he didn't put gel or mousse or any kind of product in it. His eyes were bright, and he had no bags under his eyes. About six foot three, he slouched in the plastic chair in the interview room, though he clasped his hands together like a schoolboy. Fenway sat down across the table, placing a yellow legal pad and pen in front of him.

"I hear you'd like to make a statement, Mr. Wilkenson."

Chad straightened. "That's correct."

"And what statement would that be?"

"At approximately four fifteen P.M. today, January twenty-seventh, I was working in the supply room at the Monument Brotherhood Temple."

"Supply room?"

"It's about twenty feet down the hall from the ballroom. I heard loud voices coming from the ballroom. When I came to investigate, I saw Frank Mortimer and Ben Nichols standing in the middle of the room. Frank was holding a hunting knife straight out in front of him. I heard him say that he was going to stab Ben."

"Then what happened?"

"Ben grabbed a scepter that was lying on the floor. He hit Frank over the head and Frank dropped the knife."

"Hang on," Fenway said. "What direction was Frank facing?"

"It happened very quickly," Chad said. "I don't remember a lot of the details."

"And what did you do?"

"I left the room."

"Did you call the police?"

"I intended to, but I panicked. I must have frozen. The next thing I knew, the police were in our hallway." He nodded at Fenway. "You and the other lady officer."

"The sergeant," Fenway said. "Where did you go when you left the room?"

"Back to the supply room."

"What else can you tell me?"

"I don't remember anything else."

"We didn't find a hunting knife. Do you know what happened to it?"

"No."

"Did you go back into the ballroom?"

"No."

Fenway leaned back and scratched her head. "So you're telling me you walked into the ballroom, witnessed Frank Mortimer threaten Benjamin Nichols with a knife, then you saw Benjamin grab a scepter on the floor and hit Frank over the head, but you can't remember which way Frank was facing, and you don't know where the knife went."

"That's correct."

"And you remember nothing else?"

"I've never seen anyone get killed, Miss Stevenson. It was quite traumatic." He looked up at Fenway and met her gaze with an odd intensity. She felt a chill run down her spine.

Fenway cleared her throat. "How well did you know Mr. Mortimer?"

"I have said all I'm prepared to say at this time."

"But you did know him from the Monument Brotherhood."

"I have said all I'm prepared to say at this time."

"Were you aware that he and your, uh, leader—the whatchamacallit, the Grand Master—"

"High Worshipful Master."

"Right, that. You realize that he and Mr. Mortimer worked at the same company."

"I have said all I'm prepared to say at this time."

"You led Sergeant Roubideaux out of the building, and your friends locked the door, preventing her—and our CSI team—access to the crime scene. That's obstructing a police investigation."

"I am not the one who locked the building. As you just said, I was talking to the officer outside the building. I could not have locked it."

"I thought you weren't prepared to say anything else."

Chad scowled, then his face went impassive again. "I'm merely pointing out a fact that your officer was witness to."

"Who locked the building?"

"I have said all I'm prepared to say at this time."

Fenway leaned forward and rested her elbows on the table between them.

"Okay, Mr. Wilkenson," Fenway said, sliding the legal pad over in front of Chad. "Write down what you told me, then let's get you back to the break room so we can interview your colleagues."

"We are brothers in Monument," Chad said. "We are not colleagues."

"Aww, that's sweet." Fenway leaned back in her chair. Chad wrote at a determined, even pace, with legible if juvenile printing. Halfway down the page, he lifted the pen and stared at Fenway.

"Done?"

"Yes."

"Sign and date below, please."

Chad did so, and Fenway turned to the one-way mirror and nodded. A moment later, Deputy Salvador came into the room, led Chad to his feet, and walked him out.

Fenway waited a minute, counting the seconds in her head, then grabbed the legal pad and walked out of the room and into the observation room. Dez stood, arms crossed, gazing into the empty room.

"What do you think?"

"I haven't seen anything that rehearsed since my niece's fifth-grade play."

"Light on details, for sure. You think he's lying?"

"We'll see."

A moment later, Celeste Salvador brought Benjamin Nichols into the room. He was about Fenway's height, just shy of six feet, and his straight blond hair was parted on the left, falling just over his forehead. He was rail-thin, with watchful brown eyes and a curl to his upper lip that was almost a sneer. Benjamin sat at the table, leaning forward, but hands folded just like Chad's had been.

Fenway ran her hands over the stubble on her scalp, then shook out her hands, grabbed a fresh legal pad, and left the observation room. She went back into the interrogation room. Benjamin looked up and his lip curled further.

"Benjamin Nichols?"

"Ben."

"Your friend was just in here, accusing you of killing Frank Mortimer."

Ben didn't even blink. "Chad must be mistaken. I did not engage with Frank."

"Okay," Fenway said. "What statement do *you* want to make?"

"At approximately four fifteen p.m. today, January twenty-seventh," Benjamin began, "I was working in the supply room at the Monument Brotherhood Temple."

"Wait—*you* were working in the supply room?"

"That's correct. It's about twenty feet down the hall from the ballroom. I heard loud voices coming from the ballroom. When I came to investigate, I saw Frank Mortimer and Travis Foxwell standing in the middle of the room. Frank was holding a hunting knife straight out in front of him. I heard him say that he was going to stab Travis."

Fenway ran a hand over her face. "Do you know Chad told us this exact story? Except he was the one working in the supply room, and Frank was arguing with you, not with Travis."

Benjamin cocked his head. "I'm not sure what you mean."

"Just what I said. This exact same story, only he changed the names."

"I don't know what to tell you, Coroner. All I know is what I saw."

"Did you see where the knife went?"

"No. I haven't finished—"

"We're done here."

"Aren't you obligated to take my statement?"

"Let me guess," Fenway said, exasperated. Then she took a deep breath. No. If she finished the story for Benjamin, that could be fodder for an appeal—assuming there was ever a trial and a conviction. "Never mind, I'm not going to guess. Please continue."

"Travis grabbed a scepter that was lying on the floor. He hit Frank over the head and Frank dropped the knife."

"What direction was Frank facing?"

"It happened very quickly," Benjamin said. "I don't remember a lot of the details."

"Of course," Fenway said, tapping her fingers on the table. "Why didn't you call the police?"

"I intended to, but I panicked. I must have frozen. The next thing I knew, you and the other Black female policeman were in our hallway."

Fenway ground her teeth. "Where did you go when you left the room?"

"Back to the supply room."

"What did you do back in the supply room?"

"I don't remember anything else."

"You don't remember *anything* else? No other details? Was Travis facing you or was he turned away from you?"

"I can't recall."

Fenway leaned back and stroked her chin. "So you're telling me you walked into the ballroom, witnessed Frank Mortimer threaten

Travis Foxwell with a knife, then you saw Travis grab a scepter on the floor and hit Frank over the head, but you can't remember which way Travis was facing."

"That's correct. I've never seen anyone get killed before. It was quite traumatic." Benjamin kept his head down, staring at his clasped hands.

Fenway knew how Benjamin would respond, but she had to ask anyway. "How well did you know Mr. Mortimer?"

"I have said all I'm prepared to say at this time."

Fenway pushed the legal pad in front of Benjamin.

"Okay, Mr. Nichols. Write down what you told me, sign and date at the bottom, then let's get you back to the small conference room so we can interview your colleague."

"We are brothers in Monument," Benjamin said.

"Right, right," Fenway said with a wave of her hand. "One big happy family."

Dez held the two legal pads in front of her in the observation room. "Exactly the same story," she mused. "The names are different, but other than that, it's exactly the same."

"Do we even need to get Travis in here? He's just going to repeat what they said—only I'll bet he says Chad killed Frank. A big ol' circle of death."

"And we don't have a shred of evidence to prove otherwise. If we arrest one of them for murder, one of the others will testify to his innocence." Dez rubbed her temples. "ADA Pondicherry will never bring this to trial."

"But we don't even think any of them did it. It's just a ruse to get attention off Northwall."

Dez nodded. "Right. While we're in here playing Whack-a-

Mole, Redmond Northwall is probably gassing up his plane right now, getting ready to leave the country."

"Do we refuse to take Travis's statement? We don't have any physical evidence linking Northwall to the murder. We have the shape of the blunt object, and a theoretical bloodstone scepter that possibly matches it—that's a lot of *ifs* and *probablys*." Fenway sighed. "I guess we hope the judge signs the warrant for the Northwalls' home and that we can search it before any Brotherhood judges get their grimy little injunction hands all over it."

Fenway's phone rang—Sarah was calling. Fenway tapped *Answer* and put it on speakerphone.

"Dez and I are here, Sarah. Any news?"

"Frank Mortimer booked a one-way flight a couple of weeks ago —LAX to Belize City. For both him and Haley Sinclair."

"Belize isn't quite the Caymans," Dez said, "but not bad."

"Not bad? Why do you say that?"

"Not a bad choice for an embezzler, I mean. Belize banking legislation assures strict confidentiality. And the United States doesn't have a financial exchange agreement with them."

The door to the interrogation room opened and Celeste led in a man roughly Chad's height with a similar haircut, but he was clean-shaven.

"See?" Dez said. "He and Chad could be brothers. Shave Chad's goatee off..."

Fenway blinked. "Hang on," she muttered, tapping the browser on her phone.

"What is it?"

"Frank Mortimer's wallet hasn't turned up yet, right?"

"Right."

"So why take a wallet off a dead Monument Brotherhood member inside the temple?" Fenway pulled up the DMV photo of Frank Mortimer. "Bald. Eyes set fairly far apart. A pointy nose. Now look." She tapped her screen and a news photo of Redmond Northwall appeared. "What if he shaved his face and head?"

"He'd have to get brown contacts."

"Which you can literally buy off-the-shelf at Marks-the-Spot."

Dez pressed her lips together. "Are you saying that Redmond Northwall is impersonating Frank Mortimer?"

"I bet," Fenway said, "that if you called Piper Patten at McVie's office, she'd be able to find a list of accounts with large deposits in the last month or so. I bet she could link one of them to Frank Mortimer in about two hours." Fenway looked up at Dez. "I bet Frank Mortimer siphoned millions of dollars off Radical Familiar over the last five years. And Northwall killed Mortimer to either get it back…"

"…or to live the rest of his days under an assumed name, on the beach with a pretty girl and millions of dollars," Dez finished.

"And the crazy thing," Fenway said, "is that without a body—and if a man calling himself Frank Mortimer resurfaces in Belize—there's officially no murder. Even if we uncover the financial crimes and we somehow get the paperwork to extradite 'Frank Mortimer' back to the states, Northwall can just grow his hair and beard and go under 'Redmond Northwall' again. He could get all the money out of Mortimer's account—and we couldn't touch him."

"The perfect crime," Dez said.

"It's never perfect. He'll overlook something."

"I'll call Piper Patten as soon as I'm off with you." Sarah's phone dinged. "Oh—hang on."

"What?"

Sarah looked at her screen then sucked in a breath. "Frank Mortimer just checked into his flight."

CHAPTER SIX

"WHILE OUR INVESTIGATORS ARE LOOKING THROUGH THE garage," Fenway said, holding out the signed warrant to Emma Northwall, "I wanted to tell you that your husband was detained for questioning an hour ago at Los Angeles International Airport."

"With that whore," Emma said under her breath.

"There was a ticket for the young woman, yes, but she didn't appear to be at the airport and hasn't yet checked in for her flight. We've got a deputy heading over to Nidever University to see when she was last there."

"He usually keeps things he doesn't want me to see hidden in a long gun box that's up in the rafters in the garage."

Fenway tilted her head.

"We've been married for twenty years, Coroner. Very little gets past me." She set her jaw. "Of course, I didn't find out about the missing money and the girl he was screwing. I guess he still had ways to hide things."

Fenway took out her radio and pushed the button. "Deputy Salvador, look for a long gun box hidden in the rafters."

"Above the Porsche."

"Above the Porsche," Fenway repeated.

"Roger that." Celeste's crackly voice came through the radio.

"I went upstairs to the guest bathroom earlier," Emma said, "and I found all kinds of hair in the sink. Gunk from shaving cream, too. He'd shaved—it looked like a lot more than just his beard, too." She frowned. "And left me to clean it up."

"I'm sorry," Fenway said. "But this will all be over soon."

"Over?" Emma scoffed. "It won't be over. This is just the first phase. He'll go on trial. I'll lose this house—I'll lose everything. I've got to go to the dealership later to see if I can sell my car—and that Tesla—just to get enough money to pay my bills this month." She balled her hands into fists. "What am I going to do? I've volunteered for all sorts of organizations in the last twenty years, but I haven't held a paying job. And with our name dragged through the mud, who'll want to hire me?" She sighed. "You know what else I just found out—because it just came through to my email?"

"What?"

"He sold his entire stake in Radical Familiar."

"But—I thought it was a private company."

"He still owned thirty percent. He just sold his stake to an investment group out of Montreal. The deal was finalized this morning. Eight million dollars—a fraction of what it was worth." She tapped her chin. "Although after the news gets out that Frank stole twenty-three million dollars from them, maybe it won't be worth so much."

"Frank stole *twenty-three million?*"

"I knew something was going on," Emma said. "I thought at first he was looking to trade me in for a newer model."

"That's why you hired the private investigator?"

"Oh, you know about the P.I.? Yes, that's right. But it seemed like more than an affair. He was being very secretive about everything. His precious little Monument Brotherhood meetings were lasting longer, and he was having more of them."

"It looks to me like he was trying to catch Frank red-handed."

The radio buzzed. "Coroner, we found something."

Fenway glanced up at Emma. "Excuse me for a moment."

"Certainly, certainly."

Fenway walked outside into the dark night and across the driveway to the garage. The open door spilled light out onto the gravel. Dez was staring up into the rafters, where Celeste sat. She handed down a large gun box.

"This could hold a shotgun," Celeste said, "but it's not nearly that heavy."

Dez grabbed onto the gun box, and Fenway rushed over and grabbed the other end.

Together, they laid it on the concrete floor—probably where the Tesla usually parked.

"There's no lock," Fenway mused.

"Maybe he needed the lock for something else, and he figured if he was going out of the country, he'd be safe enough with this hidden somewhere he thought no one would find it."

"Maybe." Fenway flicked the metal tabs and opened the case.

Inside, a long metal staff—titanium? Silver? Maybe just plated with a precious metal. It glinted with glory, even in the dim light of the garage.

And at the top of the staff, like a giant gaudy engagement ring, sat an emerald-cut stone, about five inches square. Yes—that could have made the wound Fenway had seen in Frank Mortimer's skull.

Wherever his body was now.

The stone was a deep green, almost black, with orange-red flecks so large they looked like paint splotches.

"The Bloodstone Scepter," Dez said.

Fenway pointed to a brownish-red splotch on the side of the

stone. "Not just the Bloodstone Scepter," Fenway said. "The murder weapon. I need to get my fingerprint kit."

"I've got one in the cruiser," Celeste said.

"Thanks. That'll work."

Dez's phone rang. She looked at the screen, then turned and walked out of the garage. Fenway pulled on a pair of blue nitrile gloves as Celeste went out to her cruiser to get the kit.

Dez walked back in. "Redmond Northwall will spend the night in L.A. county jail, and he'll get transferred up in the morning."

"No sign of Haley Sinclair?"

"Not at LAX. Callahan just called from Nidever. She's in her apartment off-campus."

"She never went to Los Angeles with Redmond?"

"It appears not."

"What does she have to say for herself?"

"Do you want to pull her in for questioning tonight? It's past nine o'clock."

"I don't know. Can we arrest her?"

"On what charge?"

"Obstruction?"

"What exactly did she obstruct?"

Fenway nodded. "You're right. Let's ask for her to come in for questioning tomorrow."

Dez paced around the garage. "I'm not sure how long we can hold off the feds on this one."

"Murder trumps identity theft, doesn't it?"

"Traveling on someone else's passport is a federal offense. A big fine, up to twenty-five years in jail. They're not messing around."

Celeste walked back into the garage and handed Fenway a black plastic fingerprint kit case.

Fenway set the case down on the garage floor, then lifted the Bloodstone Scepter out of the gun case and placed it gently on the garage floor. She didn't want to transfer any of the blood to any other surface, but fingerprints were more important. Besides, there was plenty of blood on the gemstone to get DNA and a blood type.

She realized she'd been holding her breath and exhaled long and slow. She opened the case and removed the fingerprint dust bottle and the brush.

Celeste watched over her shoulder as Fenway began tapping the bottle, the dust shaking out slowly over the shaft of the scepter.

But nothing stuck.

Fenway took a deep breath and slowed down. After the adrenaline of the day, she had to remind herself to be careful, to be deliberate, to go slowly. She hated dusting for fingerprints in front of an audience, but at least Celeste was being quiet.

Still nothing. No fingerprints at all.

"Celeste," Fenway said, "what do you know about the Bloodstone Scepter? Do the people who use it wear gloves? Maybe something ceremonial?"

"I don't know." Celeste paused for a moment. "I spent a little time this evening researching bloodstone."

"Yeah?"

"Not a lot—but I wondered if it had any significance to the murder."

"*Is* there significance to the bloodstone?"

"It represents purification and vitality, or according to some people—let's see, how did they phrase it—'noble sacrifice.'"

"Noble sacrifice? From what I know about Frank Mortimer's embezzlement, there was nothing noble about it."

"Some religions believe the red splatters in the stone represent the blood of Christ."

"Yeah, I've heard that last one."

"And there are others who think it clears out negative energy."

"Hmph." Fenway spun the scepter so she could dust the other

side of the shaft. "Seems to me that whoever hit Frank Mortimer with this thing was expressing a *lot* of negative energy."

Again—no fingerprint dust stuck. She sighed.

"No prints?" Celeste asked.

"I'm afraid not." Fenway pushed herself to her feet. "There isn't a single fingerprint on the staff part of the Bloodstone Scepter."

"Maybe the killer wore gloves."

"I'll tell you something—Chad, Brad, and Tad weren't telling the truth."

Celeste nodded. "I saw the notes from the interview. Same answers, different people to blame it on."

"That's right. But no one mentioned gloves. No one was wearing gloves when we were at..." Fenway trailed off.

"What is it?"

"They didn't want us in the temple," Fenway said.

"Right."

"We assumed it was one of the cleaning staff who called 9-1-1."

"That's what I heard, too." Celeste paused. "The call was tracked, wasn't it?"

"I already asked Sarah," Fenway said, taking out her phone, tapping the screen, and putting it on speaker.

"Hey, Fenway," Sarah answered.

"Still at your desk?"

"For now. I'm about to call it a night."

"I'm in the Northwalls' garage with Celeste. Any luck tracing that 9-1-1 call?"

"Not if you call a prepaid phone lucky. I was able to track it to the store where it was purchased. I've got a call into them—maybe we'll get a break with credit card receipts."

"But it was a member of the cleaning crew?"

"Uh—I think that was the dispatcher's assumption."

"Man or woman?" Fenway asked.

"The dispatcher?"

"No, the caller."

"They didn't identify themselves," Sarah said. "The voice was high-pitched. The dispatcher thought it was a woman—and since there aren't any female or non-binary members of the Monument Brotherhood—"

Celeste shot a quizzical look at Fenway. "Does it raise your suspicions at all that it's a burner phone?"

"Not that uncommon," Sarah said. "If the cleaning crew member is living paycheck to paycheck, a prepaid phone makes sense. Or if they're undocumented."

Fenway was silent.

"Everything okay?"

Fenway shrugged, even though Sarah couldn't see her. "Something's bothering me, but I can't put my finger on it."

"Don't you have this case all but wrapped up? The rich software CEO found out his CFO was stealing millions of dollars, killed him, stole his identity, and decided to run off to Belize with Frank's money and a pretty girl." Sarah chuckled. "It's not even that original."

"Still," Fenway said, "I think this was a murder we were never supposed to know about. One day Frank Mortimer is here, the next he's gone—and Redmond Northwall appears under Frank's name in a country without a financial crime agreement with the United States."

"How would you explain the disappearance of Redmond Northwall?"

Fenway paused. "He would have taken over Frank Mortimer's life in Belize."

"Right," Sarah said quickly, "but if he's living as Frank *there*, then how does he explain what happened to him here? Surely people will notice when he stops showing up to work."

Fenway furrowed her brow. "I'm not sure."

"We can ask him," Celeste piped up, "when he gets to Estancia for questioning tomorrow morning."

"Maybe Haley Sinclair can shed some light on Redmond's motive," Fenway said. "But that burner phone is still bothering me. You're looking into it?"

"I don't expect a lot of other information," Sarah said. "I'm fairly certain it was purchased with cash—that's another thing you can count on."

"You don't think it's the killer trying to throw us off the scent?"

"If it is, they're doing a pretty good job of it." Sarah paused for a moment. "Maybe I should have contacted you earlier. I wanted to have all the information before I called."

"No, no, Sarah, that's fine." Fenway scratched her scalp. "I'd hoped that we could find whoever made the call and interview her." She paused again. "Still..."

"What is it?"

"The order of events makes it seem like it was—I don't know— unplanned. Like the cleaning crew just happened to..." Fenway trailed off again.

"Is everything all right?"

"Sarah," Fenway said, "can you find out who the cleaning crew is? If they use an outsourced company, and when the building is scheduled to be cleaned?"

"I hope the Monument Brotherhood doesn't keep that information as secret as the rest of their organization's details."

"Do what you can." Fenway paused. "And it can wait until tomorrow morning."

"Aww, and I was just settling in," Sarah said. "I've made a note— I'll do it as soon as I get in tomorrow."

———

It took about half an hour to clean up the garage. Fenway went into the house.

"Emma?" she called from the large tiled entryway.

Emma's face appeared at the top of the staircase. "Are you finished?"

"Yes. I'm sorry we had to stay so late."

"Did you—did you find what you were looking for?"

Fenway nodded.

Emma paused. "You said earlier he was traveling with that girl."

"I said her name was on the second ticket," Fenway said, "but no, she wasn't with him. She never checked in for the flight."

Emma's brow furrowed. "I see."

"You seem disappointed."

"I don't know—I expected if he was leaving me, he'd be going with her." A smile touched the corners of her mouth. "Perhaps she didn't want to leave her cushy life here and travel with an old man to Belize."

Fenway grinned. "You'd think all that money would be reason enough, but I suppose anyone can change their mind."

Emma cleared her throat. "I appreciate you telling me, Coroner."

"You're welcome. I'm sorry you had to go through this."

"What happens to my husband now?"

"They'll transport him up from L.A. tomorrow," Fenway said.

"Will I need to come down to the station?"

"I'm not sure yet. Can we contact you?"

"Certainly. I believe I gave the deputy my cell number."

Fenway nodded. "I'll get out of your hair now. Have a good night."

Fenway left through the front door and closed it solidly behind her. She squeezed her eyes shut. What was it that didn't make sense?

She walked down the stone path to the street, pulling out her phone. 10:43. It might be too late to call McVie, but with their abandoned dinner plans, she figured she should chance waking him up.

He picked up on the first ring. "Oh, hey. I didn't think I'd hear from you tonight."

"I wasn't so sure either. Is it too late to come over?"

"I think I can make time in my busy schedule."

"You're not working late?"

"Nope—you'll never guess who called me this evening to tell me my services are no longer required."

"Emma Northwall."

"Ha. Right you are. How did you know?"

"We can talk more when I get there," Fenway said, unlocking her car and opening the door. The Accord still smelled faintly of tacos.

———

"So," McVie said when he opened the door, "Was the Emma Northwall guess just lucky, or did you have information that I didn't?"

Fenway walked into McVie's apartment. "I'll just say that it would be hard for you to follow her husband around when he's in jail." She pulled McVie's face down to hers and kissed him on the mouth.

"Hi," McVie said.

"Hi yourself. I'm glad you didn't have to work all night."

"Me too."

Fenway angled her head up and kissed McVie again. "I missed you."

McVie closed the door to the apartment. "You know, I don't

have to be at work until, like, ten. We could sleep in." He pulled Fenway close, his hand on the small of her back. "Or something."

Fenway groaned. "I have to be at the sheriff's office early. They're bringing Redmond Northwall up from L.A. in the morning."

"So, does that mean he's your killer?"

Fenway paused.

"Uh oh," McVie said, pulling away slightly.

"What do you mean, uh oh?"

"He's your primary suspect. All the evidence points to him. And yet..."

"And yet," Fenway repeated, breaking from McVie's embrace. "Yeah. I think this was the perfect crime. A man steals millions from his company; the CEO finds out, kills him, then steals his identity. By this time tomorrow, he would have been sipping a rum punch on the beach with millions of dollars. And no one would have suspected him of murder, because everyone would think he's the person who he killed."

"So, what's throwing it off for you?"

"Redmond Northwall controls every single aspect of his life," Fenway said. "He's got his schedule down to five-minute chunks. He's not only the CEO of where he works, he's the Grandmaster Flash of the Monument Brotherhood, too."

"Most Worshipful Master."

"Whatever—the point is, he needs to be in control. And you would think that if he were planning the perfect murder, he would know that the cleaning crew would be there—and he'd either alter his plan or alter the cleaning crew's schedule."

"Maybe he did, and someone didn't get the message."

"I suppose it's possible," Fenway said. "I just wish we could talk to the person who made that 9-1-1 call."

"Anyway, enough work talk."

Fenway grinned. "You planning on distracting me?"

"For a little while, anyway. Tomorrow morning is going to come mighty quick."

Fenway elbowed McVie in the ribs, then went into the bedroom, McVie following.

CHAPTER SEVEN

Sarah opened the door of Fenway's office. "Haley Sinclair just arrived at the sheriff's office. They're putting her in the interview room."

"Great," Fenway said, glancing at the clock on her PC. "Redmond Northwall arrive from L.A. yet?"

"Not yet."

"Probably a good thing. We don't want Haley and him to coordinate their stories."

Sarah gave Fenway a wry smile. "As if they haven't already."

Fenway put on her jacket and picked up her purse. "We'll see."

The walk across the street was short but surprisingly chilly. It hadn't rained, but the fog that had settled over Estancia on the late January day made the concrete walkways slick with mist.

Dez was already in the interview room, a manila folder in front of her. A young woman with pale skin and strawberry-blonde hair sat across from her. The woman turned her head to look at Fenway with her large hazel eyes.

Fenway had seen Haley in McVie's investigation photos, but the picture hadn't captured the intensity of the young woman's gaze. No wonder Emma Northwall was so agitated by Haley's presence in her husband's life.

"Did I miss anything?" Fenway said.

"Just keeping Miss Sinclair company until you arrived," Dez said.

"I have class in an hour," Haley said, still staring at Fenway.

Fenway moved out of Haley's glare, and sat in the metal chair next to Dez. "Honestly, Miss Sinclair, I think you'd better plan on getting notes from a classmate. We've got a murder to solve, and your name keeps coming up."

"My name?"

"That's right."

Haley turned her attention to Dez. "I don't know anything about a murder."

Dez didn't meet Haley's eyes, instead opening the folder in front of her and pulling out a photo of Frank Mortimer.

The photo was of the face of a supine Mortimer, eyes closed, skin pale, the backdrop a metal table.

Haley recoiled.

Dez placed another photo on top of the face of the dead Frank Mortimer: the photo from the Phillips-Holsen hotel of Haley in the white dress, embracing Frank.

Haley glanced up at Dez, then looked over at Fenway.

Dez took out a piece of paper from the folder: a copy of the hotel receipt.

"Frank Mortimer met you in a hotel two weeks ago," Fenway said. "We have more photos of the two of you getting in the elevator together. Anyone can see that his intentions were, well, amorous, shall we say? The embrace in the hotel lobby seems to suggest that the feeling was mutual."

Haley stared down at the table.

"Sergeant," Fenway asked, trying to inject as much curiosity into her voice as possible, "Do you have the picture of the car that dropped off Miss Sinclair?"

Dez pulled another photo out of the folder: it was another snapshot from McVie, this one of Redmond Northwall's Tesla, with Haley's face behind the passenger window.

"Last night," Fenway said, "the driver of this car was arrested at LAX, getting on a plane to Central America with the dead man's passport."

"I don't—" Haley stopped and took a deep breath. "I don't see what that has to do with me. Those pictures were taken two weeks ago. We're both consenting adults. If his wife had anything to—"

"The thing is," Fenway said, "there was a ticket for the seat next to him under your name."

Haley was silent. Then, cautiously, she said, "I didn't know that he'd bought a ticket for me."

"You didn't know?"

"No." Haley looked Fenway in the eyes. "I wouldn't have said yes if he'd invited me, and I wouldn't have showed up even if I *did* know about it."

Fenway sat back in the chair and watched Haley closely. The young woman dropped her eyes to the table. Fenway ran a hand over the stubble on her scalp, then leaned forward and rested her elbows on the table.

"I need the truth, Miss Sinclair."

"I *am* telling the—"

"The *whole* truth. The things coming out of your mouth are technically true, but you're intentionally misleading us."

Haley leaned back and bit her lip.

"Maybe you didn't know for a fact that he'd purchased a ticket for you, but you suspected he had a seat reserved for you next to him. Maybe you never said 'yes' to his invitation to run away with him, but you made him think you'd be there. And maybe you didn't have any intention for him to wind up dead, but you know a lot more than you're letting on."

Haley raised her head and stuck her jaw out. "Maybe I need to talk to a lawyer."

Fenway looked at Dez. "With what we have right now, could we charge Miss Sinclair with anything?"

"Obstruction," Dez said.

The color drained from Haley's face. "But—I haven't *done* anything."

"You can sort that out with your lawyer."

"Wait," Haley said. "I—I need to be in class."

Dez stood up quickly and smacked her hand on the table—the loud thwack made Haley jump. "Miss Sinclair, this is a murder investigation. A man is dead. The owner of the car who dropped you off? They arrested him for stealing our murder victim's identity. You better start talking, or you'll be missing a lot more out of your life than just one class."

Haley gripped the edge of the table, her knuckles white. "I was just trying to get his money back."

"Whose money?" Dez pressed.

"Redmond's," Haley blurted. "I mean—Redmond's company. Frank had been stealing money from Radical Familiar for years. At least—at least that's what Redmond said."

"So," Dez said, "you and Redmond hatched a plan to get his money back? You seduced Frank as part of the plan?"

"Not exactly," Haley said, her ears turning red.

"Then what, exactly?"

Haley covered her face with her hands, then lowered them to the table, her eyes unfocused. "I do some cosplay work on the side —dress up as superheroes, villains, anime characters, that kind of thing. I did a shoot for a Radical Familiar ad campaign in costume, and Redmond came up to me after the shoot. At first, I thought he was just another old guy hitting on me, but he tells me he has a business opportunity he wants me to get in on."

"Which was?" Dez asked.

"He told me Frank had stolen millions of dollars over the years from the company. He found out it was being siphoned into a bank account in, uh, Panama or Guatamala or something."

"Belize," Fenway said.

"Right—that's it. Belize." Haley ran her hands through her strawberry-blonde hair. "So I was supposed to meet Frank at a dinner party. Flirt, get his number, pretend I'm interested."

"That was all? No information gathering?"

"No. I just needed to get him alone."

"Why the hotel?" Dez said. "Was that your idea?"

"No, Frank suggested the hotel." Haley shrugged. "I didn't ask."

"So Redmond drops you off for your hotel rendezvous?"

"Right. I insisted he come right from work. That way, he'd have his laptop with him." She stared down at the table. "We went up to his room and we had a drink. And—uh, he fell asleep."

"You put something in his drink?"

"Some people just can't handle their alcohol," Haley said quietly.

"Fine." Slipping drugs into Frank's drink wasn't important anyway—at least not right now. "So, what did you do when Frank was unconscious?"

"I got into his laptop."

"How did you break in? Did you have his password?"

Haley held up a finger. "I had his fingerprint right there. And he was out cold."

Fenway nodded. "What did you do once you were on his laptop?"

"I opened his browser and logged into his account in—uh, did you say Belize?"

"Right."

"Yeah. I went to his transaction history and copied everything—all the information of the money transferred into his account."

"Was this on your own?"

Haley's eyes went wide. "No, no—this was all at Redmond's direction."

Fenway nodded. "And Redmond paid you to do this?"

"Yes. A lot more than I usually get from a cosplay appearance, I'll tell you that. It made a nice dent in my tuition payment this semester."

"How did you obtain Mortimer's bank account information?"

"A program I ran from a USB drive," Haley said. "Redmond said it was all the info they'd need to catch him and fire him."

"You got the program from Redmond Northwall?"

Haley looked down at the table and studied her fingernails.

"So why the plane ticket?"

"Well—uh, Frank woke up a little later."

"You didn't just leave?"

"Redmond didn't want Frank to suspect anything. So Frank woke up. I—I'd taken his clothes off and put him into bed, and when he woke up, I made it seem like we'd had sex. I, uh, you know, complemented him a lot. Told him he knew how to make a girl feel like a real woman."

Fenway rolled her eyes.

Haley chuckled. "Yeah, it was cringe, but he loved it. I told him I had to get back to campus, but that I'd like to see him again."

"And did you?"

"I wasn't going to," Haley said, "but Redmond said he wasn't sure they had everything. I went to dinner with Frank a couple of times after that. He asked me—" Haley paused, squeezed her eyes shut, then opened them again. "He asked me if I wanted to go to the Caribbean with him."

"After a week?"

Haley nodded but looked worried. "I was laying it on thick. Wasn't the first time an older guy asked me to run away with him."

"And what did you say?"

"Uh, well, to be honest, I panicked. I didn't tell him no, but I didn't tell him yes, either."

"What *did* you say?"

"I told him I loved the Caribbean, and I might have said something like 'why go to college and work all your life to retire to the beach if I can just live on the beach right now?'"

"So he thought it was a yes. Even though you didn't *technically* say yes."

Haley squeezed her eyes shut. "I guess so."

Dez looked at Fenway, and they both stood up. "Hang tight, Haley."

"I didn't do anything wrong," Haley said. "I helped stop someone from stealing money."

They walked out of the room, into the hallway, and closed the door. "What do you think?" Fenway asked.

Dez shook her head. "The girl's putting on an innocent act— and mark my words, it *is* an act." She walked to the vending machine along the hallway and held her card up to the scanner, a bottle of water dropping. "The things she's done are morally questionable. Some of them might be illegal—using Mortimer's fingerprint to access an account that isn't hers, for example."

"But if it's not an account at a U.S. bank, can we even arrest her?"

Dez shook her head. "We'll have to talk to ADA Pondicherry. I think the way she accessed the account is against a federal statute, but if her intent was to return stolen money from a foreign bank account, I'm not sure the U.S. Attorney will agree to charge her."

"I'd rather not involve the Feds more than we have to." Fenway bit her thumbnail in thought. "What about an obstruction charge?"

Dez chuckled. "It'll never stick. And she seems like the kind of person who'd know a lawyer competent enough to sue the department for wrongful arrest."

"We just let her go?"

Dez shrugged. "She's not the one who was traveling on someone else's passport."

"At least we have Redmond Northwall on the hook for that—even if it's only a federal crime."

Dez made a low growling noise in the back of her throat. "I looked into that statute—it's not clear if it'll be enforced. Usually for illegal entry into the States, and this isn't an INS issue." She crossed her arms. "I'm afraid Northwall's lawyers will negotiate a big fine and a watered-down sentence. He'll get sixty days in a country club facility and then be back to running his company."

"So we need to get him on the murder. That's our jurisdiction. And we can make sure he goes to prison for a long time." Fenway shook her head. "But I still don't feel like that's justice—the money's gone. It's already in an account in Belize. People at Radical Familiar will lose their jobs—they'll lose everything."

"We're not going to take it out on Haley Sinclair," Dez said. "I suspect beneath that innocent act, she has a cruel streak. I know she enjoyed toying with the rich white-collar criminal, but she's not who we're after." Dez opened the bottle of water and took a drink. "Doesn't mean we can't put a uniform on her, though. See if she goes back to her apartment, or if she meets with anyone."

Fenway tapped her foot. "Should we bring Redmond Northwall through while we're taking Haley out?"

Dez pursed her lips. "I don't know if that's a good idea."

"It'll let us see how involved Haley is. If he thinks she was supposed to meet him at LAX, for one. He might say something. Give her a look, even. It might give us something to go on."

"As long as we don't do anything to put her in danger. He's a powerful man—and our top suspect for killing Frank Mortimer. You don't think he'd do the same for a woman he thinks betrayed him?"

Fenway nodded. "All the more reason to put a uniform on her."

———

Ten minutes later, Fenway waited in the hallway while two sheriff's deputies walked past the vending machine, one on either side of Redmond Northwall.

The door to the interview room opened, and Haley Sinclair walked out, followed by Dez.

Northwall's eyes narrowed. "You!"

Haley's eyes widened, then she looked down at the ground.

"Where were you?" His voice rose and echoed down the hall.

Haley stepped behind Dez as they passed Northwall and the deputies.

"You can't hide," Northwall shouted, turning to glimpse Haley as the deputies walked him into the interview room. "This is on you!"

The deputies pushed Northwall into the chair facing the one-way mirror.

"I'm not done with you!" he shouted after her.

One of the deputies locked Northwall's handcuffs to the rail on the table in front of him and walked out of the room.

"It was her!" Northwall yelled. "It was her—not me!"

The deputy closed the door.

Fenway sighed and walked into the observation room. On the other side of the one-way mirror, Northwall stared straight ahead, a furious look on his face, then after a moment, his murderous gaze softened, and he buried his face in his hands.

Dez opened the door of the observation room and walked in, carrying a folder, and stared at Northwall through the one-way mirror. "On one hand, that worked better than expected. On the other hand, we've definitely got to put her under protective custody. Who knows what he'll do to her?"

"It's good that we know that now," Fenway said. "I'd bet he started having thoughts about her being at fault as soon as he realized she wasn't showing up at the airport."

Voices outside in the hallway. Then the interview room door opened and a familiar—if unwelcome—face walked in: Lynn Hayes, the lawyer who'd arrived at the Monument Brotherhood Temple.

She set her briefcase on the table, took a seat next to Redmond Northwall, leaned in and spoke in low tones. He nodded once, then after listening for another moment, nodded again.

Ms. Hayes glanced up at the one-way mirror. "Ready when you are," she said in a confident, controlled voice.

"This should be entertaining," Fenway said.

CHAPTER EIGHT

"Before you go in," Dez said, "they confiscated Northwall's laptop at LAX. We got it this morning."

"Have we found anything on it yet?" Fenway asked.

"Encrypted hard drive, but Northwall had the password written in a notebook in his bag. Gotta love old-school solutions to modern-day problems."

"Did the warrant come through for his cell phone?"

Dez nodded. "And Judge Harada signed a warrant for a number he's called a total of ninety-seven times in the last four weeks. It's a burner, but we can get any unencrypted texts or numbers that it called too. We might have it by tomorrow."

"Great." Fenway stretched her arms above her head. "Do we want to make them sweat a little before we go in?"

The observation room door opened, and a man, about four inches shorter than Fenway, stepped in. He was about thirty-five, with close-cropped hair and a goatee. Wearing a tailored three-piece black suit with a purple-and-gray striped tie, the man carried a thick manila folder. He nodded at both of them. "Sergeant. Coroner."

"ADA Pondicherry. To what do we owe the pleasure?" Dez asked.

Pondicherry opened the folder and turned to Fenway. "Even without a body, I believe we can get a grand jury to indict Northwall for murder. And if we get a judge to hold him without bail—"

"No way, Vel." Dez put her hands on her hips. "Half the judges in Dominguez County belong to the Monument Brotherhood."

"One of them signed an injunction overturning our search warrant of the temple," Fenway added.

"I've asked Emma Northwall to come in," Pondicherry said. "If I can get her to talk with him—"

"You don't know if they're working together," Dez said.

Fenway shook her head. "After what Emma said to us? How she's losing everything because of the money he stole? I don't think so. In fact, I think he'll react to his wife the same way he did to seeing Haley in the halls—he'll scream at her and tell her it's all her fault."

Dez cocked her head. "You don't know that—maybe he *does* think it's Haley's fault."

"Let's go in and see what they have to say," Vel said.

"Are we prepared to arrest him?" Fenway asked.

Pondicherry nodded. "We'll take our chances with the grand jury." He sighed. "And with the judges. I'll see if we can get someone assigned who isn't connected to the Brotherhood." He opened the door, and Dez and Fenway went out first. Fenway took a deep breath and opened the door to the interview room.

"Finally," Lynn Hayes snapped. "My client was unlawfully detained—"

"You've met the two of us before," Dez interrupted. "I'm Sergeant Roubideaux, and this is my boss, the County Coroner.

And this"—she indicated the man in the suit—"is Assistant District Attorney Vel Pondicherry."

"Your client," Pondicherry said, "was caught at LAX attempting to board an international flight on another person's passport. That violates federal law—"

"You're not the feds," Hayes interjected.

Pondicherry raised his eyebrows. "You might be unaware that your client committed a felony punishable by a large fine—and up to twenty-five years in prison."

"Ten." Hayes set her jaw. "There's no way you'll prove Mr. Northwall's intention was for terrorism purposes."

"Still," Pondicherry said, "that will give us plenty of time to make our murder case."

"I didn't—" Northwall began.

Hayes held up her hand. "Don't say anything, Red." She turned to the ADA. "The passport was a simple mix-up. I'm sure there are plenty of people in Estancia who would be more than willing to vouch for Mr. Northwall's character. A judge might fine Mr. North-wall, but for an honest mistake like this?"

"I happen to know the U.S. Attorney," Pondicherry said, "and fleeing the country with funds stolen from your company won't be looked at as an honest mistake."

"I'm willing to take that chance," said Hayes.

Pondicherry cocked his head at Northwall. "Are you willing to bet the next ten years of your life on that, Mr. Northwall, or do you want to answer some questions? This could go a lot easier—"

"I'm not saying anything," Northwall sneered. "I was set up by that little—"

"Red!" Hayes barked. "Be quiet."

"Easy for you to say." Northwall rattled his handcuffs against the table. "You're not the one sleeping in a jail cell tonight."

"My client isn't saying anything else." Hayes leaned back in her chair.

"Then you must want to play ball on the murder charge." Pondicherry opened his folder. Inside were Fenway's photos of the dead body of Frank Mortimer, including shots of his head wound.

Hayes opened her briefcase and handed Pondicherry a second folder. "You have your photos; I have mine."

The photos showed a variety of flesh wounds, including one particularly nasty open wound on Haley Sinclair's forehead. "I've got twenty photos of your supposed victim with a well-known member of the—uh, what's it called? Cosplayer community. This particular cosplayer often dresses up in superhero outfits and uses lots of makeup to make it look like she has—I don't know, radioactive poisoning, third eyes, a Viking hammer sticking out of the back of her head. We posit that this young woman was likely the architect of these supposed photos."

"The coroner and the sergeant are more than willing to testify that Mr. Mortimer was deceased at the time of examination—and in their subsequent questioning of Mr. Northwall."

"Let's see who the judge believes, then. I believe we could pull the Honorable Michael Haggarty."

Pondicherry set his jaw. "Haggarty needs to recuse himself. Mr. Northwall holds a position of power over him in a local social organization."

Hayes cocked her head. "As soon as you provide documentation showing this organization's power structure, we'll stipulate to the recusal."

His nose twitched. "What do you want, Ms. Hayes? I'm not a monster. I'd love to hear an alternate theory of the crime. Do you want to provide us with another—"

"I want my client to go home to his family."

Pondicherry glanced at Fenway, but Fenway gave a small shake of her head.

"Give us a moment." Pondicherry opened the door and he, Dez, and Fenway stepped outside into the hallway.

"I don't like this," Dez murmured.

Pondicherry kicked at the linoleum floor with the toe of his right dress shoe. "If we let him go," he said, "Northwall will be on the next plane out of here."

"So arrest him for murder," Fenway said.

"Hayes is itching to file a motion to dismiss with prejudice," Pondicherry said. "The problem is, I think if we get the wrong judge, he'll get it."

"Then let the Feds take him on the passport charge."

Pondicherry frowned. "I know the U.S. Attorney. This statute is used almost exclusively to catch undocumented workers. A rich white man traveling to the Caribbean with his girlfriend? We'll be lucky if he even gets fined. Why do you think he's still in our custody?"

Fenway folded her arms. "Well, by all means, we should just give up, then."

Dez exhaled. "No one's saying that, Fenway."

Fenway turned to the ADA. "When was he detained? Last night?"

Pondicherry looked at his watch. "We have forty-eight hours to hold him without formally charging him. That means we have a little over a day to get something on him."

"Doesn't look like we have many other options." Fenway tapped her chin. "We could try applying a couple different kinds of pressure. One—financial. He has all his money in an account in Belize. If we freeze his accounts here, we can guarantee he can't buy a plane ticket to get out of the country."

"Unless he has rich friends in some sort of secret society."

Fenway grunted. "It's better than nothing, I guess, but it won't be effective." She looked up at Pondicherry. "What about his wife? Sure, they don't get along, and sure, he was leaving the country with another woman—"

"Is this reverse psychology?" Dez asked.

"—but if we bring her in," Fenway continued, "we can listen in on their fight. You know guys like Northwall are just dying to say something—anything—to twist the knife in. It might give us a place to look for more evidence, maybe even find the body."

"If they don't have an underground incinerator at the temple," Dez muttered.

"I like that you're thinking laterally," Pondicherry said, "but so far I haven't heard anything that keeps Northwall locked up. It might delay his trip by a few days, but he'll be dipping his feet in the Caribbean by the weekend—and with all the millions of dollars in the account in Belize."

Fenway nodded. "Then we have twenty-four hours to find something else to make the murder charge survive the arraignment."

———

An hour later, Dez and Fenway drove down the streets in the Northwall's neighborhood. Fenway tapped her phone.

"Would you put that away?" Dez pulled next to the curb in front of the Northwall's large house.

"There might be some additional financial pressure we can put on Northwall," Fenway said.

Dez put the transmission into Park. "We're here. And that's good news, as long as Northwall stays in the country."

Fenway got out of the Impala and looked up at the house. The enormous garage lay closed and silent behind the Italian cypresses.

They walked up the stone footpath to the front door, and Dez reached out to ring the bell.

Emma answered the door a moment later, her hair up in a high ponytail and in a tank top and yoga pants. She frowned when she saw Fenway. "Well, it happened. All the money's out of the checking account. He screwed me just like he screwed the company."

"We're so sorry, Mrs. Northwall."

Emma scoffed. "After this, you better believe I'm changing my name back."

"Of course." Fenway cleared her throat. "Your husband is at the sheriff's office in Estancia."

"Hmph."

"We believe he murdered Frank Mortimer."

"Great," Emma said, hands on her hips. "What does this have to do with me?"

"He's transferred all of his funds overseas, and it's hard to get it back." Fenway woke up her phone and read off the screen. "But when those funds are gained through murder, sometimes the foreign banking agency will release the money back to their rightful owner."

"That's me."

"Some funds are, I'm sure. But some of them may have been stolen from Radical Familiar."

Emma exhaled. "It probably won't keep me afloat very long," she said, "but I suppose every little bit helps."

"The thing is," Fenway said, "the evidence against your husband is thin."

Emma folded her arms. "Are you asking me to testify against him? I'll run out of money long before this ever goes to trial."

Fenway shook her head. "Spousal privilege—you can't testify as to any communication between the two of you."

Emma scoffed. "I probably wouldn't be useful anyway. He barely talked to me for the last two years." She paused. "What is it you're asking me to do, exactly?"

"Come down to the station. He'll be in holding tonight—but we have to let him go tomorrow unless we get more evidence against him. And if we don't, he'll be out of the country in a day or two."

"With my money," Emma muttered.

"With all the money he stole," Fenway said. "So—you know how to push his buttons? To get him to start saying things just to, uh, you know—"

"Rub it in? That he's rich and I'm worthless? Oh, yeah, I can get him to say that."

"Do you think any of the things he might say would give us a clue how he committed the murder? Or where we could find evidence?"

Emma looked down at her white athletic shoes. "I'm not sure— let me think." She looked up. "But—surely you found the murder weapon. And doesn't it match the body?"

Fenway shifted uncomfortably from foot to foot. "Well—" She glanced at Dez, who gave a slight shrug. "That's the problem. We don't have the body."

Emma's eyes went wide. "What do you mean, you don't have the body?"

"It was—" Fenway's eyes darted to Dez again, but the older woman had cast her eyes down. "There was a legal issue."

"It's still at the temple?"

"We have photos," Fenway said quickly, "but if you can help us get some additional evidence, you can help us overcome the, uh, lack of a body."

Emma gritted her teeth. "He just gets away with everything, doesn't he?"

"Not if I can help it," Fenway said.

"Nor I." Emma dropped her hands to her side. "So—you need me to show up at the sheriff's office tomorrow?"

"Eight o'clock, if you can."

Emma's brow creased. "That's awfully early. Can you do nine thirty?"

Dez stepped forward. "Do you want your money back or not?"

Emma's eyes widened. "Of course. Eight o'clock it is."

———

"How real are our chances of getting this money back from the accounts in Belize?" Fenway closed the door of the McVie Investigations office and turned to Piper.

Dez stepped around Piper's desk and narrowed her eyes at Fenway. "You mean you said that to Emma *without* knowing if you could actually get the money back?"

"Hang on, I'm thinking," Piper said. She pushed her chair back from her desk and rested her chin on her fist. "There's *no* chance if Redmond Northwall doesn't get indicted, so it's better than nothing."

"It's our best chance," Fenway said.

"Uh…" Piper glanced up at Fenway and creased her brow. "It's not your *best* chance."

"Our best *legal* chance."

"Again," Piper said, "this is a gray area. The money was illegally obtained in the United States and put into an account in Belize. You were hoping to convince the authorities in Belize to release the funds back to their rightful owners if the owner of the account is arrested for murder."

Fenway crossed her arms. "Right—but we don't know if the account belongs to Frank Mortimer or Northwall. What happens if it belongs to Mortimer?"

Piper sucked in air through her teeth. "I won't say it's impossible to get it back, but the bank will probably hold the money until they get a death certificate. Well—a death certificate they'd *accept*. It's unclear whether one from the United States would meet their requirements."

"Let's assume they'd accept a U.S. death certificate."

"Then the money would get paid out to any beneficiaries listed on the account."

Fenway looked at Dez. "Do you think it's possible Mortimer put beneficiaries on his account? He probably wouldn't want his wife to get the money."

"His kids are grown," Dez said. "Don't they live on the east coast?"

"Right." Fenway rubbed her chin. "I suppose they might be convinced to pay the rightful owners back."

"Or," Dez said, "what about Haley Sinclair? Mortimer planned to run away with her."

"You think *Haley* would have been the beneficiary?"

Dez shrugged. "She told us she laid it on thick."

Piper rolled her chair back in front of her computer. "Once I find the account, I can see if there are any beneficiaries listed." She began to type, her fingers flying on the keyboard.

"What happens if there are no beneficiaries?"

Piper shook her head. "It might go to his wife, but since she doesn't live in Belize, it could get into some thorny legal areas I don't understand. My Spanish is pretty good, but not the legalese stuff. I could ask Migs, though."

Fenway and Dez were silent, watching the screen over Piper's shoulder.

A banking screen came up. Fenway squinted. There were a lot of transactions—and a lot of numbers in the seven figures.

"There's good news, better news, and bad news," Piper said.

"The good news is, I found Frank Mortimer's account. And the better news—you don't have to deal with the beneficiary question."

"And the bad news?" asked Dez.

"There's no money in Mortimer's account."

"What?"

She clicked again. "Hang on a minute—no, I'm right. All the money was transferred to a different account at the same bank."

"Who does that account belong to?"

"A string of numbers in the ID area. I'll figure it out. Give me just a second."

"It's got to be Redmond Northwall's account, right? How long will it take?"

"I don't know." She clicked on a command line interface screen and began typing.

"Haley used a USB drive on Mortimer's laptop," Fenway said. "Maybe that'll help you track the accounts? She said it was a program that Northwall gave her."

Dez clicked her tongue. "No, she didn't. You asked her if it was a program that Northwall gave her, and she didn't answer."

"Right, but..." Fenway trailed off. "I took that as an implied *yes*, thinking Haley didn't want to get herself into trouble by admitting she used malware."

Dez nodded. "But maybe it *wasn't* an implied yes. Maybe she got the program from somewhere else."

Piper drummed her fingers on the desk. "There was a hacking competition a couple of months ago—a white hat thing. One of the runner-up programs was an anti-fraud banking application. After the money disappeared from a legitimate account, it would track those financial transactions, authenticate them, and move the stolen funds to an escrow account." Piper clicked onto a browser and brought up a page with a CyberBankingHero logo at the top.

Fenway furrowed her brow. "How do you know this?"

Piper shrugged. "Had to keep myself busy while Migs was studying for the bar. Now, hold on." Piper typed furiously and several screens came up. She zoomed in on one of the screens, full of code, then clicked on a banking screen, opened another screen of code, and studied that. "Of course," Piper murmured. "Why didn't I see this before?" She typed again. "Okay—here it is." Piper pointed at the screen. "Yes. That's Redmond Northwall's account. This is the bank account in Belize that all of Frank Mortimer's money was transferred into."

"So Redmond stole back all the money Frank took from Radical Familiar?"

Piper screwed up her face. "But instead of returning the money to the company, it looks like he kept it for himself." She tapped the screen. "Some of the electronic markers on the online transfers here. Someone with impressive computer skills did this."

"Redmond Northwall is the CEO of a software company—he has computer skills."

"Hacking skills, Fenway. Northwall might know his way around a spreadsheet, but I bet he wouldn't know a SQL injection from a hole in the ground."

Dez cocked her head. "You think whoever wrote that white-hat banking program did this?"

Piper nodded. "And I'm looking at the code from the Cyber-BankingHero site. She submitted it under the handle SinCitySuper."

"Wait—she?" Fenway asked.

Dez scratched her chin. "Isn't Haley getting her masters in computer science?"

"Some of these time stamps, some of the comments left in the scripts? I don't have concrete proof, but I think SinCitySuper is Haley's handle." Piper turned to Dez, and she pointed at the screen. "And I think *she* initiated all these bank transfers. Mortimer's accounts were altered with a script that matches the date and time when she was in the hotel room with Frank Mortimer."

"Maybe the U.S. attorney *will* be interested in prosecuting after all," Fenway murmured.

Piper turned back to the screen. "Now I get how she could take Frank's money without him even getting a red flag that it was being siphoned off." She pointed to the screen. "See? This bank is running an old version of the database tools. There's a script she ran…" Piper's voice trailed off as she clicked on another screen. "Oh. Open port—and that gave her access to the alerting tools. Brilliant. Let's see how she got the money deposited in Redmond's account." She clicked onto another window, then stamped her feet and squealed.

"What's wrong?" Dez asked.

"What's wrong is that I'm not nearly as good as she is." Piper looked at the screen and sighed moonily.

"No—I mean what's wrong with Redmond's account where he put all the stolen money?"

Piper cackled, then clicked the window for the ledger statement for the bank account. "Plenty, if you're Redmond Northwall and you're expecting twenty-five million dollars in your account." Piper zoomed the screen in on the last number in the ledger.

$0.00.

CHAPTER NINE

Fenway's jaw dropped open. "So—where did the money go?"

Piper giggled. "I have no idea."

"This isn't funny."

"Oh, Fenway, but it *is*. Didn't you say Redmond Northwall cleared out all his accounts and was leaving his wife penniless?" Her eyes sparkled. "It's almost a shame he *didn't* get to Belize only to find he had nothing."

"Where did it all go?"

"My guess is some account that SinCitySuper controls."

Dez furrowed her brow. "But—Haley was in *class*. The girl steals twenty-five million dollars and you mean to tell me she's not quitting school and partying in a penthouse in Vegas?"

Piper shrugged. "Maybe she wants to finish her degree first."

Fenway shook her head. "How did she think we wouldn't be able to find this? Do we have enough evidence to arrest her?"

Piper shifted in her seat. "Uh—well, you can't actually use anything I just showed you."

"What?"

"This is all stuff protected by international agreement. Belize's banking statements aren't admissible in U.S. courts." Piper cleared her throat. "And all the stuff I just showed you was *highly* illegal if I'd done it to a U.S.-based bank."

"What?" Fenway repeated faintly.

Piper crossed her arms. "You wanted answers. I gave you answers."

Fenway looked at Dez. "So why did Redmond blame Haley for everything?"

"I figured it was just because he knew she was the one who initiated all the transactions," Dez said.

"So when he was arrested at LAX, he figured she'd betrayed him," Fenway said. "And now he's trying to throw all the blame on her."

Dez folded her arms. "The transactions might have been illegal, but Frank Mortimer initiated the original fraudulent transactions to his account in Belize. If Northwall did anything, it was all outside the country. We have no jurisdiction there."

Fenway shook her head. "So the money's gone, Piper?"

"I might be able to locate it, but SinCitySuper is *good*. She obfuscated the name of the bank. Tokenized all the identification numbers. It might take me a couple of weeks." She tapped her chin. "Or if she used a 1024-bit hash for the tokens, I might not be able to break it at all."

Fenway smacked her hand on the work table behind her. "Emma was the one possibility we had to get Redmond to slip up and say something about the murder!"

Piper pushed herself away from the desk. "What do you mean?"

Dez gave a mirthless chuckle. "Fenway promised Emma that if she helped us catch Northwall, she could get her money back. If she can't get her money back, we have no leverage."

Piper arched her eyebrow at Fenway. "Why would you promise—"

"No," Fenway said sharply. "It was absolutely *not* a promise. I told her that there was no way we could get her money back if Redmond *didn't* get charged with murder. But I never promised her she'd get it back."

"Well, now, she won't." Dez tapped her chin. "But she doesn't know that."

Piper looked like she'd eaten something rancid. "Oh, now, Dez, that's cruel."

"We can start a collection plate around the office for Emma. Besides, if we nab Northwall, we could have *something* to show to the authorities in Belize. They might be able to take action with the bank."

Piper leaned back in her chair. "I suppose it would be worth a shot."

"We need to tell Redmond's attorney that we need to speak with him tomorrow, don't we?"

"I wanted Emma talk to him separately," Fenway said.

Dez shook her head. "She's an agent of the county in this situation. We don't tell his lawyer that she's talking with him tomorrow, they could exclude anything she says at trial—and everything else that goes with it."

Fenway made a face. "But then he won't let his guard down."

"With his wife in front of him—who's screaming about betrayal, theft, who knows what else? Might not be the most productive conversation." Dez shuffled her feet. "Besides, it's not like we have a choice. We either call Counselor Hayes, or we risk this evidence getting rejected. And we'll be forced to let him go."

———

The next morning, Fenway stared at her computer screen. She'd been reading this email for almost five minutes, the information never getting into her brain. She blinked and her eyes focused on the clock in the right corner of her screen. 8:19 A.M. Where was Emma Northwall?

The door opened, and Dez stuck her head in.

Fenway looked up. "Emma's here?"

Dez shook her head. "Frank Mortimer's body washed up on Cypress Point Beach."

Fenway jumped to her feet. "You've got to be kidding me."

Dez held up her keys. "You want me to drive?"

Fenway grabbed her purse, and the two of them rushed out of the office. Five minutes later, they were turning onto Ocean Highway heading to the Route 326 turnoff.

Fenway squinted through the window. "I suppose if Emma Northwall doesn't show—"

"You know, Fenway," Dez interrupted, "she said nine thirty. Eight was too early for her."

"But she *agreed* to eight."

A sardonic smile touched the corners of Dez's mouth as she steered the Impala into the fast lane. "That's cute. No matter how many charities she supports, she's been a rich man's wife for two decades. I'll bet you she shows up at nine forty-five, insisting that *you're* the one who told her nine thirty."

Fenway looked out the window. "I guess it won't do any harm to have Redmond stick it out in his cell another hour and a half. Especially since we need to deal with Frank's body."

"As long as we either charge or release him to the Feds by about six o'clock," Dez said, glancing at her watch. "I asked Celeste to take over for us if she gets there earlier than nine thirty."

"Or if we don't make it back in time."

Fenway took out her phone. "I could call her. See if she's still planning on coming in. Maybe make it later if she wants. That way, we don't have to rush through this."

Dez stared straight ahead. "Sure."

Fenway called Emma's number.

"You've reached Emma Northwall. If you'd like to—"

Fenway ended the call. "Went right to voice mail."

"Maybe she's in the shower. Or on the road."

"I'll try again in a half hour or so."

They turned onto Highway 326 and drove for about five miles, parking behind an ambulance.

The highway was a hundred feet up from Cypress Point Beach, with a ravine running parallel to the shoreline. Dez and Fenway navigated the steep descent via a long set of wooden steps leading down to the beach, with a footbridge over the ravine.

"I love this beach," Fenway said, reaching the bottom of the steps. "The dead body only takes away from it a little."

The body lay supine about fifty yards down the beach from the end of the staircase, and Fenway snapped on a pair of blue nitrile gloves as she approached. Two paramedics stood about twenty feet away, a stretcher next to them.

The body was still recognizable. Fenway knelt on the sand next to the corpse. She placed her hand on Frank Mortimer's cheek. "Hasn't been in the water more than a day," she murmured. "Probably less than twelve hours." She lifted her head. "Current coming from the north?"

"That's right." Dez tapped on her phone, scrolling, then was quiet for a moment.

"What are you doing?"

"Checking out high and low tides. Assuming the body didn't get caught on anything, it probably traveled about four or five miles in the last twelve hours."

"We don't know when it washed ashore."

"True." Dez put her phone down and stared out at the sea. "I guess we won't be able to narrow down where he went into the water."

Fenway blinked, then squinted. "Easy enough to weigh the body down, though, isn't it?"

"Weights could have come loose."

Fenway shook her head. "I don't see any ligature marks on the arms or legs. No distressed clothing—no stretched-out pockets where someone might have put rocks."

"So whoever got rid of the body did it in a hurry."

"Dez," Fenway said, "check the vehicles of the three gentlemen who greeted us at the temple. See what vehicles they drive. If any of them have a pickup or an SUV, see if we can match their plates to any of the cameras in the area last night."

"I'll call Sarah."

Fenway nodded.

She continued to examine the body but found nothing else of note. Fenway turned Frank's head to the side. The ocean had washed the wound of most of the blood, as one would expect from it being in the water for hours—and that had also made the shape of the wound clearer. She wished she'd brought the Bloodstone Scepter with her, but that was in the evidence locker back in the Sheriff's Office. Still, the shape was evident.

After her examination of the body, Fenway motioned the paramedics over. Once they had Frank Mortimer inside the body bag, the paramedic placed him on a stretcher and began the slow, steady walk across the beach to the wooden steps.

Dez put her phone down as Fenway stood and removed her gloves. "Sarah already got a hit. Chad Wilkenson drives a Ford F-250 pickup." She held up the phone and woke it up; a map showing Cypress Point Beach appeared on-screen. "We might not be able to narrow down the distance the body traveled from measuring the currents. But look at this." Dez used two fingers on the screen and it zoomed out. "San Sebastian Road exit about three miles up Ocean Highway." Dez pointed to the screen where the road split. "It's an easy road to drive for a big pickup, and there are two places where the road gets close to the water—and they're both secluded. I bet the body went in there." She tapped a finger to San Sebastian Road and centered the screen to where it met Ocean Highway. "There's a gas station at the exit. I've gotten camera footage from there before—the cameras cover part of the road. I bet we look at footage from last night, we see Chad Wilkenson's pickup."

"I'm still pissed off about the round-robin story they told," Fenway said. "How we knew at least two of them were lying, but couldn't arrest any of them since we couldn't prove—"

"Yes, I was there," Dez said. "But we need to get evidence of the truck before we arrest Chad."

They walked across the beach, up the steps, across the foot-bridge, and back to the Impala. Fenway stared out the window as they drove to the gas station at the San Sebastian Road exit.

———

The office at the gas station was small, and folders, mail, and paperwork had been strewn across the desk and the side table next to the guest chair. Dez had folded herself into the task chair and stared intently at the small monitor in front of her. She hit pause, and the screen froze. Dez looked up at Fenway, who stood behind her with her arms crossed.

"The technology might not be from this millennium," Dez said, pointing to the screen, "but it works. That's Chad Wilkenson's F-250. The license plate's even visible."

"Time stamp?" Fenway asked.

"11:36 P.M." Dez grinned. "Think Chad will roll on Northwall once we arrest him for obstruction?"

"It's tough for one person to move a body," Fenway mused. "It's possible one of his 'brothers' helped him out." She squinted at the screen. "It's too bad you can't see the people in the truck."

"We're lucky to get the plate," Dez said. "This video evidence might help unstick the three-way logjam with their stories covering for each other."

Fenway tapped her chin. "I assume that whoever dumped Frank's body in the ocean took it from the Monument Brotherhood Temple. First Street has a bunch of businesses that have cameras. At least one of them must have caught the F-250."

"We're probably not lucky enough to see the actual body being loaded into the truck, though." Dez said.

Fenway took a step back and bumped into a floor lamp. "Sorry." She looked up. "What about Haley?"

"What about her?"

"This SinCitySuper handle of hers—can we get her on anything? She moved the money into Northwall's account. Aiding and abetting?"

"She's already admitted to moving the funds," Dez said, "but under the guise of getting the money back that Mortimer stole." Dez hit *Play,* and the truck drove out of the picture. "Besides, we can't use any of the information Piper showed us."

Fenway sighed, then took out her phone and tapped.

"You've reached Emma Northwall. If you'd like to—"

Fenway pressed *End Call.* "Went right to voice mail again."

"She could be on the road to the Sheriff's Office. It's almost nine thirty."

The door opened and a man with a thin face and graying beard stuck his head in. "Did you find what you needed?"

"We did." Dez cleared her throat. "We'll need the tape for evidence."

The man frowned. "Oh—it's tough to get replacement tapes. How long will you need it?"

"Just long enough to digitize it. We can have it back to you in a day or two."

The man shifted his weight. "Yeah, I guess that's okay."

Dez wrote in her notebook, ripped out the page, and handed it to the man along with her business card. "That's your receipt. You don't hear from me in forty-eight hours, you call."

Fenway reached across Dez and ejected the tape from the machine.

"Surprised you knew how to operate one of those." Dez said to Fenway, giving her a mischievous smile. Then she stood and addressed the man. "Thanks for your cooperation."

He stood to the side, and they passed him, walking into the main store, then continuing outside.

"What now?" Fenway asked. "Shouldn't we go to Chad's house, impound his truck? If he put the body in a carpet or something, the wrap might still be in the back of the pickup. We could get DNA that matches."

"Chad's probably at work." Dez took her phone out of her purse. "Let's see... Chad Wilkenson." She frowned. "Oh—I misspelled it. Hold on." She tapped a few more times, then held the phone out for Fenway to see. "Accountant at Hardy Nichols."

"That's in the business park off State Street." Dez unlocked the Impala with her key fob.

"I'll call CSI in San Mig. They should get their lab ready." Fenway paused. "And I'll call impound, too. Get Chad's truck towed to our lot."

"Do it fast," Dez said. "We don't want another cease-and-desist order from Judge Haggarty."

As Dez drove her Impala into the parking lot of the business park, Fenway squinted through the passenger's window, searching for a black Ford F-250.

"There." Fenway pointed at the pickup in the fourth row of cars.

Dez swung her Impala around and pulled into a space about fifty feet away, then killed the engine. Fenway looked up; the county's blue-and-yellow tow truck drove into the lot.

Dez got out of the car first, Fenway quickly behind, snapping on a pair of gloves. The tow truck stopped behind the F-250, and the roar of the diesel engine changed to a lower pitch.

The driver's side door opened, and a figure dressed in blue coveralls jumped onto the asphalt. The figure turned; it was a woman with an olive complexion, about five-eight, hair hidden by a *Dominguez Tow* baseball cap.

Dez grinned. "Shay—long time."

The woman broke into a grin. "Desirée—how you doing? It's been what, five years?"

Dez cleared her throat. "Closer to fifteen. But who's counting? I thought you were in Spokane."

Shay shrugged. "Bethany and I didn't work out."

"How long have you been back?"

"About six months." She cocked her head. "You still with Michi?"

Dez shot a furtive glance at Fenway. "It's complicated."

The grin returned to Shay's face. "It was always complicated with you, Dez."

Dez pointed at the F-250. "That pickup isn't complicated. We believe that truck was used in the commission of a felony last night."

Fenway rushed over to the bed of the F-250 and looked inside. It was empty—if a carpet or any other sort of makeshift body bag had been in the back of the pickup, it was gone now.

"Hey!"

Fenway cast her gaze across the parking lot.

A white man with a mustache and goatee, wearing a light blue dress shirt, a navy striped tie waving over his shoulder, came running out of the building. "Hey! That's my truck!" As he came closer, Fenway could see it was Chad Wilkenson.

Dez chuckled. "Good, now we won't have to go looking for him."

"I'd hate to make a scene by pulling him kicking and screaming out of his workplace," Fenway said.

Dez walked halfway across the parking lot to meet him, Fenway following about ten feet behind.

"Good to see you again, Mr. Wilkenson." Dez pointed at the F-250. "That your truck?"

He hesitated. "No."

"You just told us this was your truck, Mr. Wilkenson. DMV records say this is your truck. You want to try again?"

"Fine, it's my truck."

"Where were you last night between eleven and one?"

"Home. Asleep."

Dez shook her head. "We're not off to a strong start, Chad. You lied about that being your truck. Now you're lying about where you were. We have you on video driving this truck on San Sebastian Road toward the beach."

Wilkenson paused. "Didn't realize it was illegal to drive on San Sebastian Road."

"A dead body was dumped at that beach last night, Chad." Dez said it as if it were fact. "We demonstrate how you know the victim, we show the video—you really think the D.A. will think that's coincidence?"

Wilkenson's eyes darted all around the parking lot. He turned his head to look back at the entrance.

"Who you looking for, Chad?"

Chad smoothed his mustache and goatee, staring at the office building.

Then he turned and ran.

Fenway took off at a sprint after him.

"Fenway—" Dez said, but she was ten, twenty, fifty feet away.

Wilkenson was about Fenway's height, and her strides matched his.

He reached the exit of the parking lot and turned right onto the sidewalk, his legs and arms pumping, his tie flying behind him.

Fenway was gaining.

Then a roar behind her, and Fenway turned to see Dez's Impala fly out of the parking lot. Tires squealing, the car made a hard turn and headed straight for Wilkenson.

He turned his head to glance at the Impala, and Fenway leaped forward. Her hand smacked Wilkenson's right ankle, knocking it behind his left leg, and he fell headlong onto the concrete.

Fenway rolled, her right shoulder taking the brunt of the impact on the sidewalk, and she tumbled into the grass on the parking strip.

Dez braked hard next to Chad's crumpled body, and she jumped out of the car, gun drawn. "Hands where I can see them."

Chad's face was turned away from Fenway, but she saw a drop of blood land on the concrete as he got to his knees and put his hands above his head. "I haven't done anything illegal!"

Dez pulled her handcuffs out. "Chad Wilkenson, you're under arrest for destroying evidence and obstructing a police officer."

"Obstructing a—" Wilkenson's mouth fell open. "Judge Haggarty said—"

"Haggarty isn't here," Dez said, turning Wilkenson around and cuffing his hands behind his back. She read him his Miranda rights.

Blood dripped from Chad's nose onto his shirt, which was torn at the shoulder. His trousers had dirt all down one of his pant legs.

"Now," Dez said, hauling Wilkenson to his feet, "maybe you can explain how a dead body was in the back of your pickup."

CHAPTER TEN

———————

Fenway stared at Chad Wilkenson through the one-way mirror. Dez's statement about Frank Mortimer's body being in the back of his truck had been an educated guess, but he'd reacted like he'd gotten caught.

He had a piece of gauze stuck up his nose, and his forehead was forming a lump from where he'd hit it on the sidewalk.

Fenway tapped her foot. "There's no answer at the Northwall house?"

Dez shook her head. "Celeste was just there."

"Emma doesn't like Celeste. Maybe she saw who it was and just didn't answer her door." Fenway took a step back from the glass. "I want *something* to go on before I walk in there. If Emma could have gotten a reaction from Redmond, anything that would give us a clue to how he notified Chad, Brad, and Tad that the body needed to be moved—that would give us leverage."

Dez leaned against the wall. "Northwall didn't have any opportunity to contact anyone else."

Fenway's head snapped up. "Only when he passed Haley Sinclair in the hallway."

Dez folded her arms. "You seriously think his yelling at her was some sort of secret code to get Haley to talk to Chad? To get him to move the body?"

"I guess that's pretty unlikely." Fenway paced back and forth in the small observation room. "Do you think Emma is safe?"

Dez pursed her lips. "I—I haven't thought about that."

"Redmond takes all their money, basically leaving her penniless. She'll lose her house and her car and have no means of support. She's got a marine biology degree and a volunteer job that pays her nothing, from what I can see. So Redmond knows she has nothing to lose. He was planning to be in Belize by now, away from extradition, with tens of millions of dollars." Fenway stopped, then turned to stare at Chad. "He never expected to get pulled back to Estancia. He's got to think Emma knows about his betrayal and about the money being gone. And he might know that she has enough evidence against him—for the theft, for the murder, and who knows what else?"

Dez dropped her hands to her side. "So he could want her dead."

"It's possible." Fenway narrowed her eyes. "Frank Mortimer might not have been the only body in the back of that pickup."

Dez stepped next to Fenway, glaring at Chad too. "He knows he's in trouble, but I wonder if he thinks we're onto him for more than just the obstruction charges. Maybe Chad doesn't know it was *Frank's* body that washed up on shore."

"Maybe," Fenway said, "he thinks we found *Emma's* body."

Dez nodded. "But we can't go in there asking about Emma's dead body. If Emma's still alive, Chad will know we have no actual evidence. And he'll lawyer up immediately."

"I'm surprised he hasn't yet." Fenway stepped to the back of the room next to a plastic chair. "Isn't Lynn Hayes the lawyer for all members of the Brotherhood?"

"Maybe you only get criminal representation when you're the Grand Poobah."

Fenway sat in the chair and rested her chin in her hand. "I think he's protecting someone."

"Redmond Northwall."

Fenway nodded, then blinked. "That's what I assumed—but..." She leaned forward, her elbows on her knees, and rested her head in her hands. "I'm not seeing the complete picture."

Dez tilted her head. "What do you mean?"

"Let's go through this." Fenway counted each fact off on her fingers. "We find Frank Mortimer dead in the Monument Brotherhood Temple. The murder weapon is the Bloodstone Scepter, which only Redmond Northwall has access to. He's seen putting it in his garage yesterday, where we find it, and then we capture him trying to leave the country on someone else's passport."

"A district attorney's dream come true. This is as close to a slam-dunk case as you can get."

"Except..." Fenway said, raising her head and glancing at Dez.

"The contradictory witness statements and the lack of a dead body. But now, we've got our corpse."

Fenway nodded. "Do you think it's suspicious that Frank Mortimer's body just happened to wash up on the beach this morning?"

"Lucky, maybe. It's not like Chad, Ben, or Travis would have wanted to keep a dead body in the temple for longer than they had to."

Fenway sat up straight. "You think Northwall betrayed them, too? You know, 'Monument Brothers have to stick together' but then Northwall steals twenty-five million bucks and takes off to the Caribbean?"

Dez raised her eyebrows. "Show me a person who wouldn't behave the same way in that situation." She pointed to Wilkenson through the one-way mirror. "Chad put his ass on the line for Redmond. He helped push law enforcement out of the temple, he lied to the police, then he got stuck having to dispose of a dead body—all while the one man who was supposed to be his spiritual guide tries to flee the country with a woman half his age. If I were Chad, I'd be pissed off."

Fenway stood. "You don't think he's protecting Northwall. You think he'll turn on him."

"We might have to plead him down to a lesser charge, but yes."

"Destroying evidence is already a misdemeanor."

"So is obstructing an officer," Dez said, "but we could also charge him as an accessory to murder. It isn't a slap on the wrist. That's years of prison. A felony charge would wreck his career, his standing in the community—he'd lose everything."

Fenway nodded and strode toward the door. "Then let's see if he wants to play ball."

———

"We have you and your truck on video," Dez said, leaning across the table and placing the folder in front of Wilkenson. She flipped it open and a photo clearly showed the F-250 and the license plate, as well as half of Wilkenson's face.

Chad bent down and stared at the photo for a moment. "You can't tell who that is."

Dez chuckled, leaned back in her chair, and elbowed Fenway playfully in the ribs. "You think any jury in California would think that's *not* you, Chad? It's your truck. You filled the tank at a gas station five miles away using a credit card with your name on it—

ten minutes before this picture was taken. Juries can connect the dots."

Wilkenson was silent.

"We already have you for resisting arrest," Dez continued. "We're running tests on the bed of your pickup truck right now. Whose DNA do you think we might find?"

Ever so slightly, his shoulders slumped.

"We plan to make the argument to keep you locked up until we get those test results back," Fenway said. "You're a flight risk. We already know you won't come quietly. So a judge would have no choice but to hold you without bail." She leaned forward, elbows on the table, and spoke softly. "Dumping the body in the ocean is destroying evidence. Resisting arrest. Kicking us out of the temple so you could get rid of the body. These are facts the jury won't be able to interpret any other way."

Chad raised his head, glaring at Fenway. But his lower lip trembled.

"Judge Haggarty might sign an injunction, but he won't put his job on the line for something so cut-and-dried," Fenway said. "You don't want to go to jail, do you, Chad?" She hesitated, then leaned forward a little more. "A good-looking guy like you? Prison—does things to a person, Chad. Your plans—house in the suburbs, a pretty wife, two-point-five children, maybe a hot young mistress in L.A. you see during the week? That's all gone, Chad."

"What—" Chad's voice came out hoarse. He coughed, then took a deep breath. "What do you want?"

"You're going to tell us who killed Frank Mortimer," Dez said.

Chad's face fell. "And what if I don't know?"

Dez brought her face close to Chad's and looked kindly into his eyes. Then she slammed her fist onto the table in front of him with a loud *thump*. Chad jumped.

"Don't feed us that bullshit!" Dez yelled. "You were in the

temple with the body. You helped get rid of the body! Are you covering for your Brotherhood leader?"

Tears sprang to Chad's eyes. "But I don't know who killed him!"

Dez looked at Chad with menace, breathing heavily. "You know what happened."

"Okay, okay," Chad said. "I lied to you before. I didn't see anyone hit Frank. Ben and I were at the temple, getting things ready for a finance meeting, and when I walked into the ballroom, he was already dead."

Dez frowned. "That sounds like another lie to me, Chad."

"No!" Chad whimpered. "I swear, I'm telling you the truth."

"Where was Redmond Northwall?"

Chad swallowed hard. "He'd just arrived. He was getting a bottled water."

"You didn't see him before?"

"Not—not really."

"Did he have blood on his clothes? His hands?"

"No! I swear, I didn't notice anything!"

"Why didn't you call 9-1-1 when you found the body?"

Chad hung his head. "Northwall came out to see. His eyes went really wide when he saw who it was." He looked at Fenway. "That's why I don't think he did it. He seemed surprised."

"But he asked you to hide the body?"

"He wanted a few minutes to think about what to do. Ben wanted to call the cops."

"You didn't call the cops?"

"I didn't know what to do. It's supposed to be a sacred space. We're not supposed to let outsiders in."

"And then what happened?"

"Then the two of you arrived."

Fenway nodded. "After you kicked us out of the temple, what did you do?"

Wilkenson hesitated. "I don't know. I was supposed to take you out the door, then Ben was going to lock everything from the inside. Redmond said he'd take care of everything else. I did my part, then I went home." He looked down at his hands.

"And that leads us to last night," Fenway said. "When you took your truck to San Sebastian Beach and threw a body in."

Wilkenson was silent.

"Where's Emma Northwall, Chad?"

He looked up and blinked. "I—I don't know."

"When was the last time you saw her?"

"Last—" Wilkenson pressed his lips together and took a moment before continuing. "Yesterday."

"You were about to say 'last night'? Did you go to her house?"

He glanced from Dez to Fenway, back to Dez, then nodded.

"And she was alive and well when you saw her last?"

Wilkenson's brow furrowed. He opened his mouth to speak, then shut it again.

"You keeping quiet because you don't want to get your friends in trouble?"

He sunk down in his seat. "I don't know who to believe anymore. I heard Mr. Northwall stole a bunch of money and was about to leave the country."

"Why was that?"

"I heard it was because he was innocent, but the police had too much evidence against him. That leaving the country was the only way he could stay out of prison."

Fenway blinked. That didn't make any sense. Who would have told him that?

Oh, it must have been the lawyer.

"No matter what Ms. Hayes told you, Chad," Fenway said, "you were only getting part of the story."

"Well, whatever. I didn't want an innocent man to go to jail." He set his jaw and looked down, mumbling. "Wasn't even supposed to wash up."

Fenway sat back and blinked. "What did you say?"

"Nothing."

"Yes, you did. *What* wasn't supposed to wash up? The body on the beach?"

Wilkenson sat back in his chair, head down. "I think I better talk to a lawyer."

"I'm sure Lynn Hayes will be delighted to spend more time in this interview room," Dez said, standing.

Wilkenson scoffed.

Fenway stood. "Oh, sorry—not your lawyer?"

"Just let me have a phone call. I'll figure this out."

Fenway and Dez walked out into the hallway and closed the door. They walked in front of the vending machine.

"Lynn Hayes isn't Chad's lawyer," Dez said. "I guess I was right—only the leadership gets the benefits of representation."

"But Chad met Emma last night," Fenway mused. "You think he—or maybe Ben or Travis—killed her on Northwall's orders? Dumped her body in the ocean too?"

Dez stared at the vending machine for a moment, then pushed two buttons and held up her debit card to the machine's scanner. "Unless he felt guilty and told Emma what was going on." A small bag of barbecue chips dropped to the bottom. "Did you get the reports from Northwall's cellphone? The company emailed them this morning."

"I'll have to look at those. Did we get the burner phone report, too?"

"I think so, but I haven't seen it. I've been a little busy with Chad."

Fenway nodded, then tapped her fingers against the wall next to the vending machine. "And what did he mean that 'it wasn't supposed to wash up'?"

"Obviously he meant Frank Mortimer's body." Dez reached into the machine and pulled out her chips. "Even if he'd dumped another body in the ocean, Frank's was the only one we found." She opened the bag.

"But on your ocean currents app," Fenway pointed out, "you could figure out that a body that washed up on Cypress Point Beach would have come from that area. I can only assume you could reverse that and figure out that if you were to dump a body there, it would likely *not* wash out to sea."

Dez chewed a chip thoughtfully. "You have to know a little about how to read these currents, though. And it's not exact. There are undertows, freak storms—hell, the body could have gotten tangled up in seaweed and a boat could have come by and dragged it halfway to Hawaii by now."

"But that's not likely."

"No—I don't have exact percentages. Maybe we should enlist an oceanographer's help."

"You don't have to have a master's degree in ocean currents to know that's not a good beach to dump a body. So why dump it there?"

"I'm not sure." Dez took another chip out of the bag and pointed it at Fenway. "And another thing. Obviously, Northwall didn't expect us to show up so soon. The 9-1-1 call—dispatch says it was a woman. But maybe Chad—or Ben or Travis—had a moral crisis and called it in, but disguised their voice so they wouldn't get caught."

"I asked Sarah to talk to the cleaning company to see if we could identify the caller. Let's see what she found." Fenway pulled out her phone and tapped the screen. "Sarah?"

"Hi, Fenway. You've been busy this morning."

"I sure have. Did anything come through on the request to the 9-1-1 dispatcher?"

"Well, it's interesting. I listened to the tape. It's a woman's voice, and we assumed she was part of the cleaning crew." Sarah clicked her tongue. "I spoke to the company that's contracted to clean, though. They only come to the Monument Brotherhood Temple on Monday, Thursday, and Saturday. So I'm not sure who made the call."

"Is there any way—uh, I don't know how to say this—any way it could have been a man disguising his voice to sound like a woman?"

Sarah was silent for a moment. "Why would you ask that?"

"We think maybe one of the young men who were at the Brotherhood Temple that day grew a conscience and made the call."

Sarah cleared her throat. "No. Categorically. That was absolutely a woman's voice. No question in my mind."

"Gotcha," Fenway said quickly.

Then everything clicked into place in her head.

Emma Northwall's words rang in her mind. *Perhaps she didn't want to leave her cushy life here and travel with an old man to Belize.*

Since the investigation started, no one had told Emma Northwall that Frank Mortimer had booked a ticket to Belize.

So Emma already knew. She knew all about Mortimer's plan to steal the money—and maybe about her husband's plan to steal it back and leave her.

Dez caught the look on Fenway's face, pausing halfway to putting another chip in her mouth. "What is it?"

"Who's got a marine biology degree and a reason to put her husband in jail?" Fenway set her jaw. "Sarah, call the Sheriff's Office and have them put out an APB on Emma Northwall."

CHAPTER ELEVEN

The door to McVie Investigations opened. Fenway thrust out the bottle of Momentos Azules Reposado in front of her. "I didn't realize this would be so pricey."

"It's a tradition in the Castaneda house when you finish something big," Piper said, taking the tequila from Fenway's hand. "Oh—you got the reposado! Migs will *love* this."

"Sure," Fenway said. "Now what did you find?"

"Going toe-to-toe with SinCitySuper isn't easy," Piper said, turning to her desk and setting the bottle next to her mouse. "Lots of obfuscation."

"But you're sure it's her?"

"In my mind? Yeah, I'm sure it's her. But I'm not sure we have anything that'll hold up in court."

"I don't know about that—Emma Northwall paid you from those accounts. It's relevant, and you've given permission."

"I'll leave that up to the lawyers, then." Piper tapped the screen. "There's a site on the dark web for fake IDs and passports that was accessed using one of the anonymized browsers that SinCitySuper prefers. Of course, the IP address was insanely hard to track, but the algorithm used was similar to a couple of other transfers I suspect are hers—"

"I know you think this is fascinating," Fenway said, "but I really just need to know where Emma Northwall is."

Piper glanced over her shoulder at Fenway, annoyed. "I was about to tell you that those transfers align with a three-million-dollar anonymous donation to Dominguez Ocean Rescue. That more than triples what they announced at the end of their fundraising dinner two nights ago." She reached out and tapped the screen again. "And a one-million-dollar donation for Ethical Hackers for Change. I don't have a smoking gun, but I'm convinced Haley Sinclair pulled the trigger on these."

Fenway nodded. "Sorry. Yes, that's relevant."

Piper clicked onto another screen. "I narrowed the new IDs down to three names: Leann Woodley, Maisy Vanderjagt, and Anne Jefferson. All would fit a white woman in her early- to mid-forties. And the fake IDs were all ordered in the last month."

"Are there any matches—"

"I'm running everything now," Piper said. "So far, no matches on commercial airlines or trains. I'm running things with charters next —private jet companies and buses. But that takes a while." She looked sideways at Fenway and grinned. "I kind of thought we could have an early lunch while we wait."

Fenway sighed. "I'm trying to catch a murderer, Piper. I don't have time for lunch."

"And I'm literally going as fast as I can. But the data can only get processed so fast." Piper tilted her head. "You know this is ten times faster than you'd be able to get information out of the county. Doesn't matter how good Patrick is—that equipment is ancient compared to mine, and I know you wouldn't even be able to get the work order processed till Friday."

"I understand, but Emma Northwall could be getting on a plane as we speak."

"She might have left before you figured any of this out." Piper paused. "How *did* you figure this out, anyway?"

Fenway stepped to the side of Piper's desk and pulled a plastic chair toward her. "It was pretty clear that after Redmond Northwall suspected that Frank Mortimer was stealing money from Radical Familiar, he didn't just want the money back—he planned on taking it himself."

"Right. That's why you thought he killed Frank Mortimer."

"But he got greedy."

Piper nodded. "Common theme."

"He didn't just want the money from the company—or cashing out his stake—he took everything out of his joint accounts with Emma, too. He made sure Emma would have nothing."

Piper scoffed. "I guess he figured leaving the country was cheaper than divorce."

Fenway pulled out her phone. "I got reports from Redmond's cell phone this morning. And from the phone he called."

Piper tilted her head. "Can I see it?"

Fenway hesitated.

"Oh, come on. All this information from the dark web—you'd never find Emma without me."

"Fine." Fenway opened the spreadsheet and made it as big as she could on her phone, then pointed at the screen. "So look, here's the date that Haley Sinclair worked that tech event for Radical Familiar."

"The day after—that's when the calls to the prepaid phone show up."

"Right. And look"—Fenway scrolled down a bit—"here's the

date Frank Mortimer booked his flight to Belize with Haley Sinclair as the second passenger."

"A ninety-three minute call from Northwall to the prepaid phone?"

"Right." Fenway looked up at Piper. "I think that's when Northwall tried to get Haley to come with him to Belize."

Piper nodded. "And until then, Haley thought she'd just been getting Frank's stolen money back to their rightful owners."

"That's my theory, anyway." Fenway flicked her finger and a second report appeared. "Because look who the burner phone called the next morning."

Piper tilted her head. "I don't recognize that number."

"Really? Look at the first report again." Fenway flipped back.

"Oh." Piper's eyes went wide. "That number is a secondary number on Northwall's account—that must be Emma's phone."

"Exactly. I think Haley told Emma exactly what Redmond was planning."

"But—that's the only call to Emma's number."

Fenway pointed three lines down. "Do you see that number?"

Piper squinted. "Yes."

"That's the burner phone that made the 9-1-1 call the day Dez and I found Frank Mortimer's body in the temple. First call to *that* burner phone is the day after the call to Emma. I think Emma got a burner phone so she and Haley could talk."

Piper exhaled. "So, you're saying that Emma got the Bloodstone Scepter—"

"From her garage, where Redmond kept it—"

"—then went to the temple, maybe got in using her husband's keys. She met Frank there, killed him with the scepter, then called 9-1-1 and she's been spending the rest of the time framing her husband for his murder."

Fenway nodded. "That's exactly what I'm saying. When it

looked like we'd have trouble prosecuting him without a body, she convinced Chad Wilkenson and one of the other Brotherhood members to 'protect' Redmond by throwing the body into the ocean. But I bet she knew currents—she works with the ocean charity, plus she has a marine biology degree. She intended for the body to wash up on shore in the next day or two. That way, we'd have what we needed to prosecute."

"And meanwhile," Piper said, "Haley—SinCitySuper—transfers all the money out of Redmond's account in Belize and into her account."

"That's right."

Piper frowned. "Why is it okay with Haley for Emma to have all the stolen money, but not Redmond?"

"I have a feeling," Fenway said, "that Radical Familiar Software will soon get a wire transfer in the amount of all the money that Frank Mortimer skimmed off the top. And Emma Northwall will be able to comfortably live on the money her husband sold his stake in the company for."

Piper's computer dinged. "We got a hit." She turned back to her screen and clicked with her mouse. "Only one of those names, though," Piper said. "Anne Jefferson is a name on a passenger manifest for a private jet headed for Guadalajara out of Estancia."

"When?"

Piper pressed her lips together. "It's scheduled for takeoff in twenty-eight minutes. I'll text you the tail number."

Fenway jumped up, pulling her keys out of her purse. "I better hurry."

———

Fenway's Accord shuddered as its tires squealed, cornering hard onto Airport Boulevard. A police cruiser streaked past her on the right, lights flashing but no sirens. She glanced at the driver: Dez.

She followed the cruiser as it turned into the private hangar area. A chain-link fence separated the parking lot from the runway. A Bombardier A300 was on the tarmac, its stairs down.

Fenway squealed to a stop in the parking lot, killed the engine and jumped out of the Accord. Dez was right behind her. They ran through an open gate and sprinted across the tarmac toward the jet.

"Stop!" Fenway yelled.

But the noise of the airport drowned out her voice. She glanced over at Dez, who was running with her badge held over her head.

A staff member in a YourJet uniform stuck her head out of the plane, then glanced at the two women sprinting toward her. She walked down the steps and held her hand up as Fenway and Dez slowed to a stop in front of her.

"Yes, ladies?" the woman said in a Dutch accent. "How can I help you?"

"You have an Anne Jefferson aboard this flight," Fenway said, trying to catch her breath. "We need her to come with us for questioning."

The woman frowned. "We had a passenger by that name, but I'm afraid there was a last-minute cancellation."

Fenway cursed under her breath.

"Daphne? Is everything all right?" A second woman's face appeared: pale, freckled features framed by red hair. Emma Northwall.

"Emma Northwall," Fenway said, "you are..."

Then she trailed off before she could arrest her.

No proof. No evidence. Everything pointed to Emma's husband —not her. All she had was conjecture. And questions.

"You're wanted for questioning regarding the murder of Frank Mortimer."

Emma smiled. "I'm sorry, Coroner, but my husband stole a lot of money from hardworking people. I'm traveling overseas to try to get it back."

"You're——" Fenway bit her lip, but there was no other way to play it. "You're wanted in connection with Mortimer's murder."

"His murder?" Emma showed shock on her face. "Am I under arrest?"

Fenway clenched her fists. She could arrest her—but for what? They could only hold her for forty-eight hours. No fingerprints on the weapon, no one to put her at the scene, no way to even connect her to the burner phone.

Dez pulled on her sleeve. "You don't have any evidence? I thought you said that Piper——"

"I thought," Fenway murmured to Dez, "we could arrest her for traveling under Anne Jefferson's passport. And then we'd build a case with everything we'd uncover in the next few days or weeks."

"I'm sorry?" Emma said, frowning, but her eyes twinkling. "Did you say Anne Jefferson? Oh no, I'd never travel under a passport that wasn't mine." She cocked her head at Fenway. "Do you know that my husband was just arrested for doing that very thing?"

Fenway's jaw dropped open.

"I'd love to help, Coroner, I really would. But I've gotten word that my husband was a thief, and I think I can do something to get that money back. After all, he and I are married—I might convince the banks in Belize to grant me access to the money, then I can return it to its rightful owner." She smiled. "And that would be a great win for the Sheriff's department, wouldn't it? Instead of going under, Radical Familiar could continue employing people, attracting investment from outside the county."

"A man was killed," Fenway said.

Emma nodded. "Yes, I knew Frank. His wife and I are quite close. A real shame how he tried to take everything from her." She sighed dramatically. "And I've heard my husband was responsible for his murder, as well. His lawyer told me. Now that Frank's body has been recovered, it's an open-and-shut case. She's recommending he take a plea. He's always been a fighter—which, I admit, hasn't been the best for our relationship—but perhaps she'll get him to see reason."

Fenway's stomach tightened.

Dez elbowed Fenway. "We have nothing," she hissed in Fenway's ear.

"She's literally getting away with murder, Dez."

"And there's nothing we can do. Let's go."

"We could arrest her."

"For what? Murder? With what evidence?"

"For—for helping dump the body. Same thing we charged Chad for—I bet she's the one who put him up to it."

"You can't prove that, either." Dez shook her head. "You'll put your career on the line just to keep her off this plane. And you'll lose."

Fenway opened her mouth, then shut it again. "I hate this."

"I do too, rookie," Dez said.

Fenway jumped as if stung. "You haven't called me that in months."

"Yeah, well, you need to learn that you can't win 'em all."

Dez turned and walked back to the police cruiser.

Fenway watched her go.

"I'm sorry," the YourJet staff member said, "but unless you have a warrant for this woman's arrest, I'll have to ask you to vacate the area around the plane so we may depart safely."

Fenway looked from the staff member to Emma's face.

"I'm sorry, Coroner," Emma said. "This is a horrible situation for everyone involved. I'm doing what I can to make it better. I'm sure you understand."

"I understand perfectly," Fenway said, hearing the note of bitterness in her voice. Then, attempting a modicum of sincerity: "I hope you get the company's money back."

Emma nodded.

Fenway turned and took a few steps, then turned again to say something to Emma.

But the door was already closed.

CHAPTER TWELVE

"You're really stressed out tonight," McVie said, eyeing Fenway across the table at Dos Milagros.

"Yeah, well, it's official—I let a murderer go." She'd ordered three tacos instead of her usual two, and her first bite of the lengua was tender and spicy and perfectly balanced as always. And it tasted like cardboard.

"That was two weeks ago."

"And yet I'm still pissed off about it."

McVie nodded. "You said you got a postcard?"

Fenway wiped her hands off on her napkin, then dug in her purse and pulled out a postcard. *Galápagos Islands*. The front had several pictures: beautiful trees, the ocean, sea turtles. She turned it over and noted the red Correo Aéreo stamp.

Dear Miss Stevenson,

I must apologize for misleading you during your investigation. By now, you've doubtless seen that the money is back with Radical Familiar, and that Frank Mortimer's personal money has been distributed to his wife. She will no longer lose her house or retirement savings. Maybe that can be a small comfort to you.

Best regards,

Emma

Fenway flicked the card over to McVie. "How often did this happen to you when you were sheriff?"

"You've got to remember that Harrison Walker wasn't nearly as diligent as you are. Dez and Mark closed a fair amount of cases. We maybe had half a dozen murders in the time he was coroner. About half were domestic cases, and it was clear who was the killer. The other half? People fighting over drugs. There was a home invasion. We never solved those—we never had a prime suspect, either." McVie took a bite of his carnitas burrito. "Look at the bright side: because of you, an innocent man won't spend the rest of his life in jail for a murder he didn't commit."

Fenway swallowed with difficulty. "He *will* spend ten years in federal prison for his passport issues. The U.S. attorney wanted to prosecute after all. Set an example, I guess." She took a drink of her horchata. "Probably some prison with a golf course and chef-prepared meals."

"Ten years, huh?"

"Well—the judge might give him ten. My guess is he gets out in five and he's running another tech company as soon as he's released."

"But he won't be running the Monument Brotherhood."

"No." Fenway took another bite. She'd seen the news article that morning: The national organization had pulled its association with the Central Coast chapter. The most powerful people in the chapter were either dead or in prison, and the building was up for sale. Fenway wondered if Emma had anything to do with that—maybe she'd ask Piper when she saw her again.

McVie picked up the postcard. "You're mad you had to give the case to the Feds."

"No, no." Fenway gave a slight chuckle. "Maybe a little."

He turned the postcard over and read the back. Then he returned it to Fenway, shaking his head. "When I was sheriff, if I didn't solve an embezzlement case, it meant that I couldn't help the victims. Maybe a family would miss their rent payment, or a single mom would lose her car and wasn't ever getting it back. At least the employees of Radical Familiar still have jobs."

Fenway sighed and took another bite of her taco. The taste came back—at least a little.

"And Emma Northwall paid on time—and in full," McVie said wistfully.

"Her house is on the market," Fenway said. "I saw the listing. Four and a half million."

"That'll go a long way in Ecuador. Or wherever she is."

Fenway took a drink of horchata. "I just wish I could arrest Haley Sinclair for *something*. The feds would be interested if I could figure out what might stick. If it weren't for her—"

"Then Frank Mortimer would be sitting on a beach with twenty million dollars in the bank and Radical Familiar would have had major layoffs." McVie took another bite, then talked with his mouth full. "Haley is more hero than villain, Fenway."

"She operates in a gray area."

McVie gave Fenway a sad smile. "Maybe you need some rum in that horchata."

Fenway looked up at McVie. "Maybe I do."

CAST OF CHARACTERS

Fenway Stevenson: A former nurse practitioner with a master's degree in forensics, she moved to Estancia in April after her mother lost her battle with cancer. Fenway has a rocky relationship with her father. First appointed to fill out the coroner's term, she was re-elected two months ago.

Her family and friends

Craig McVie: The former sheriff of Dominguez County who lost the mayoral race in November. Recently divorced, he officially started dating Fenway after the election. He now owns his own private investigation firm.

Nathaniel Ferris: The richest, most powerful man in the county, the oil magnate founded and owned Ferris Energy, which he recently sold to a competitor.

Piper Patten: Formerly in the county's IT department, this willowy redhead is a whiz at forensic accounting and data gathering. She likes the command line interface almost as much as she likes her boyfriend, Migs. She now works for McVie.

Co-workers and law enforcement personnel

Sergeant Desirée "Dez" Roubideaux: A detective in the coroner's office, Dez has worked for the county for 25 years. She's a dedicated, determined investigator despite her wisecracks.

Sarah Summerfield: Fenway's administrative assistant, she works in the coroner's office.

Deputy Celeste Salvador: A sheriff's deputy and friend of Fenway's.

Vel Pondicherry: The assistant district attorney in Dominguez County.

Victims, suspects, and witnesses

Frank Mortimer: The CFO of Radical Familiar, a hot technology company, he is found murdered on in the temple of the Monument Brotherhood, where he was a member.

Redmond Northwall: The CEO of Radical Familiar is also the High Worshipful Master of the Monument Brotherhood.

Emma Northwall: Redmond's wife is on the board of a local environmental charity.

Haley Sinclair: A grad student in the computer science

department at Nidever University, Sinclair is known for her cosplaying at comic book conventions and other events.

Chad Wilkenson, Benjamin Nichols, and **Travis Foxwell**: Members of the Monument Brotherhood who are in the temple at the time Frank Mortimer's body is found.

Lynn Hayes, Esq.: The attorney for the Monument Brotherhood.

Paul Austin Ardoin's fortnightly newsletter:

http://www.paulaustinardoin.com

Subscribe to Paul's Patreon, with several levels of members-only goodies:

https://www.patreon.com/paulaustinardoin

I hope you enjoyed reading this book as much as I enjoyed writing it. If you did, I'd sincerely appreciate a review on your favorite book retailer's website, Goodreads, and BookBub. Reviews are crucial for any author, and even just a line or two can make a huge difference.

ACKNOWLEDGMENTS

Many thanks to my editor Theresa Baumgartner and to my cover designer Ziad Ezzat of Feral Creative. This book is much better because of you.

Thanks to my patrons, including J.W. Atkinson, Sandy D'Alene, Stan Peters, Janice Webber, and Donna White, and to my early readers and reviewers.

Special thanks to Cheryl Shoults, who has been invaluable creating, organizing, and maintaining my author newsletter, website, reader teams, promotions, and a million other items.

To my wife, my children, and my mother: I'm deeply grateful for your encouragement and support.